KEL   Kelly, Galen G.
         The Rasputin Club

KEL   Kelly, Galen G.
         The Rasputin Club

The Rasputin Club
Copyright
Galen G. Kelly, 1996
Kingston, New York

Copyright acknowledgments:
  "Sunset Grill"
  "Puttin' on the Ritz"
  "White Rabbit"
  The Quick Red Fox - John D. MacDonald
  The Return of Sherlock Holmes - Sir Arthur Conan Doyle

ISBN: 1-57745-060-4

Library of Congress Catalog Card Number: 99-72363

This book is dedicated to an operative code-named
Mongoose.
He was a killer of serpents.

And to

Michael John Kelly
1915 - 1996

PREFACE

"Without Rasputin, there could have been no Lenin."
Alexander Kerensky

The men met in a small but elegant apartment high above New York's Fifth Avenue. The stark medieval furniture complemented the room's decor, which was designed to represent a cloistered monastery. The windows, which would have looked out over the modern metropolis, had been sealed. Piped in were the quiet sounds of Gregorian chants; the faint smell of incense completed the atmosphere. The meeting room was in marked contrast to the modern themes found in the rest of the apartment.

Twelve men sat on wooden benches around a heavy, plain wood table. Since almost the turn of the century, the men of the Council had met like this. Through the years the Council Chamber moved from country to country and place to place but the traditions and, above all, the need for secrecy and anonymity remained the same. Only death by natural or other causes removed one of the twelve. Whether replaced by a son or another carefully selected candidate, once appointed, they became faceless shadows moving through history, appearing only when necessary to advance their single goal.

Today all were dressed in expensive dark business suits. The tall man at the head of the table spoke.

"Then if all present accept the financial report, I move to close this meeting."

"Just one more thing," interrupted a heavy-set man. "I have to say I am concerned about these people we have hired..." he paused, searching for a word.

"To clean up our messes," interjected a man across the table.

"No. To assist in advancing our goals," corrected the tall man at the head of the table.

"I don't want to quibble over words," the heavy-set man said. "It's just that after all these years we have finally come so close."

"That's right," said the man across the table. "Maybe it's time to get a little ruthless. Too often we've played the dilettante.

"I know all that," answered the heavy-set man, "but hiring people like these, well, it's sort of like entering into a pact with the Devil."

"It's a little late for that sentiment," volunteered a voice from the far end of the table. "There are those who would say we already have."

The meeting closed with the familiar, brief, and seemingly ancient, ritual. Then, over the next hour, individually and in pairs, the twelve men of the Council discreetly exited the building. Most hailed cabs but two entered waiting limousines. Whiting, the tall man who had led the meeting, to accommodate his adopted, pseudo-plebeian identity, walked to the subway entrance.

The heavy-set man, named Chandler, who had expressed his concern during the meeting, returned to his office in the Executive Suite of the Dunsmore International Bank. He was met by his politely impatient secretary who began to hurriedly review his telephone calls. There were calls from Hong Kong, London, Swiss and even Japanese banks. There was money to be transferred, agreements to be signed, and deals to be closed. It was decisions by men like Chandler that affected the economies of whole nations.

Alice Swanson had been his secretary for twenty years. A mature woman, she secretly suspected that he was having a romantic liaison of long duration. But a man of such power needed to be accessible twenty-four hours a day, every day of the year and, for the most part, Chandler was, but there were those times, such as today, that he simply disappeared without warning, with neither explanation or apology.

The man who had sat across from Chandler, who was not bothered by the prospect of a more ruthless approach to problem-solving, was taken by limo back to his office in the United Nations. On the way, he reflected on his comments and attitude during the meeting. He considered himself a pragmatist and, as such, he accepted the use of violence or other extreme measures as simply a means to an end. Spelle, a stern man, smiled to himself, amused by his current position at the U.N., for he was Deputy Director of Operations for Peace-Keeping Forces throughout the world.

On his subway ride back to Columbia University where he held the chair of Resident Political Historian, Whiting prepared for his meeting with the graduate student who interested him. The student, a Journalism major, showed interest and promise in foreign affairs. Whiting intended to seduce him into accepting a fellowship with a small, prestigious foreign policy think tank secretly funded by the Council. 'It was possible,' Whiting mused, 'albeit remote, that this student showed such potential that one day he might even join the Council as a member.' Whiting, the academic and philosopher, enjoyed his position of power as the principal recruiter for the organizations, businesses, and enterprises controlled and operated by him and his eleven brother Council members.

The other nine Council members returned to their offices and homes from where they controlled banks, media, government agencies, industries, schools, and any and all institutions which allowed them to anonymously exercise the power of control over almost any segment of society they chose.

PART I

THE MAN

"*I get this crazy feeling.   Every once in a while I get it.   I get the feeling that this is the last time in history when the off-beats like me will have a chance to live free in the nooks and crannies of the huge and rigid structure of an increasingly codified society. Fifty years from now I would be hunted down in the street.   They would drill little holes in my skull and make me sensible and reliable and adjusted.*"

The Quick Red Fox
McDonald

CHAPTER ONE

April 12
New York City

I wondered how long the telephone had been ringing before I picked it up. I had been in one of those deep sleeps, you know, the kind of sleep where it's more like passing out and coming to. The kind of trance-like sleep where you can't quite figure out where you are or what time it is.

"Yeah," I said authoritatively, trying to mask my confusion.

"Mr. O'Brien?"

"Speaking." I sat up, swung my legs out of bed onto the floor, and reached for my cigarettes.

"Lieutenant Wertz here, Armed Forces Police, New York Metropolitan Command. Mr. O'Brien, you're listed as the N.I.S. night duty officer." He paused as if expecting some sort of reply; not getting one, he continued. "Is that correct?"

"I guess so."

"I beg your pardon, Sir?"

I exhaled a cloud of smoke; I was coming to. "Jake O'Brien, Lieutenant Commander Naval Investigative Service, I've got the night watch. What's up, Lieutenant?"

"Well, Sir, I have a Captain Sullivan, NYPD, on the line.

Something about a dead Admiral, or something. Should I patch him through?"

OR SOMETHING? 'Jesus,' I thought! I glanced at the clock; it said 3:12 A.M.

"Yeah, go ahead, but stay on the line, and log in the call."

"Yes, Sir. Stand by." The phone went dead for a moment.

"Mr. O'Brien, I have Captain Sullivan here; go ahead, Captain." I could just picture the young Army lieutenant, so efficient, so full of energy.

"Commander O'Brien. N.I.S. What can I do for you?'

"Well, now, it sounds bad, but probably isn't, except for the Admiral, that is. Dead, dead as a door knob, he is. Morte; looks like his ticker went, heart attack. It looks like he was trying to get to a doctor when he checked out. A couple of sector cops found him. Nothing suspicious. Sorry to roust you at this hour, but I thought we should let you people know, an Admiral and all. Like to close it out before we file the unusuals." I agreed. Each morning all precincts sent a listing of all major crimes or unusual incidents down to Police Headquarters at One Police Plaza in Manhattan. Reporters checked the unusuals, as they were called, every morning. A dead Admiral with unresolved questions would attract attention. It might make the paper before next of kin was notified, something the Navy would not like.

"No problem, appreciate the call."

"Look, we have his briefcase and some personal effects; think you would be good enough to come down and sign for them?"

"Sure, no problem."

"Know where the One-Seven is?"

"Yeah, be there in about forty-five minutes." Actually, I didn't know exactly where the 17th Precinct was, but I wasn't going to admit it. It was someplace around Sixth-Eighth and Third; wouldn't be hard to find at this hour.

At least at this time of the night, there wasn't any dress code, so I pulled on jeans and a sweatshirt, grabbed my leather jacket and walked out of my building into the still-cool air of an early Spring night. I picked up a container of coffee at the all-night deli, and walked around the corner to my car.

I felt good about myself. Even after all these years I still got that feeling. The feeling of being different, of being special. In the middle of the night I could walk the toughest streets of New York in confidence. Sure, the Smith and Wesson Chief Special under my jacket had something to do with it, but it was more than that. It came with a sense of being part of the night instead of just being in it.

A well-dressed young couple coming home after a late night shot a nervous glance towards me. They were swimmers in a dark sea and I might be a shark. They couldn't tell that I was really only a dolphin.

My car was where I had left it; something to be thankful for in New York. I got in and tossed the Federal Law Enforcement Officer plate from the dash under the seat.

It only took fifteen minutes or so to get to the 17th Precinct. I parked in amongst the double and triple parked police cars in front of the building. I didn't bother to put the ID plate back on the dash - a stripped down Dodge Aries with a spot light and a bunch of antennas has got to be some kind of cop car. Besides, I didn't want to be mistaken for an FBI agent, those buckaroos not being all that popular with the NYPD

I walked into the brightly lit building; ignoring the security desk and the "Display Your Shield" sign, I saluted the Desk Sergeant in the old tradition as I passed. He nodded his head in approval. You can go anywhere provided you know the tribal customs.

I took the stairs to the Detective Squad Room on the second floor. The squad room is always on the second floor. I opened the door. In the middle of the room stood the man who had to be Sullivan - coffee cup in one hand, pizza slice in the other. He was wearing an expensive dark suit, an equally expensive loosened tie and open shirt collar. Tall, big-boned, slightly curly, thinning red hair, pot belly - a real stereotype New York Police boss.

"You must be O'Brien." His voice was deep, strong and friendly, but it also said he was used to being in charge. I nodded an acknowledgment as I crossed the room to him.

Although there were half a dozen detectives and six or seven other people in the room, including a man in a clown suit chained to a desk, no one but Sullivan seemed to see me; it was as if I were invisible. Phones rang, typewriters clicked, file and desk drawers were opened and slammed shut, papers were passed back and forth, a computer sat ignored in the corner with the screensaver fish swimming aimlessly. As a radio played 60's music, a speaker on the wall monitored the Precinct dispatcher. Organized chaos. I moved through it as an unseen ghost. Unseen by all but Captain Sullivan.

"Captain Sullivan, Jake O'Brien," I said, sticking out my hand. Sullivan couldn't figure out which to put down, the coffee or the pizza. I dropped my hand. Sullivan smiled and shrugged his shoulders. With a jerk of his head, he turned and signaled me to follow him into the one private office. With a twist of his foot, he pushed the door closed. In what seemed two bites, the pizza was gone.

Sullivan wiped his hand on the greasy napkin and extended it. "Call me Francis," said Sullivan. As we shook, he held up a coffee cup noticeably laced with bourbon. "Can I get you some real coffee?" he said, emphasizing the word REAL.

"No thanks, it's too early or too late or something."

"Okay," Sullivan began. "Have a seat, I'll tell you what we've got."

Subtly, I was being maneuvered. The moment I walked through the door the manipulation had begun. Maybe I was paranoid, maybe this was just Sullivan's style, but I figured I may as well relax and go along with the program and see where it was going. Besides, it sounded like it was going to be a long story, so I said, "On second thought, Francis, I will have some of that." I figured we were on a first name basis now.

Obviously pleased with my decision, Sullivan, with a flair, poured me half a Styrofoam cup of bourbon from a bottle in a desk drawer. Handing me the cup, he half sat on the desk, leaning over like a fat cat about to pounce on a mouse.

I was ready to confess. I took a swig of bourbon.

"Here's how I see it. This Admiral named Jeffries, Admiral Samuel Jeffries...you know him?" He asked suddenly with the sharpness of a knife.

"No, not off hand," I answered, feeling the warm relaxing effect of the Captain's special coffee. But the name Jeffries did ring a bell somewhere in the back of my mind.

"Well, okay, this Admiral Jeffries is passing through New York, see, so while he is in the City he stops by to visit some of his society friends. So he's walking down Park Avenue around 67th Street and, see, he feels a heart attack coming on. Bet he was close to retiring. You know how many guys on this job after thirty years put in their papers and drop dead? You know how that goes, kind of scary. Top off your drink?"

Like a magic trick, suddenly from nowhere, the bourbon bottle was back in Sullivan's hand and he was recharging my Styrofoam cup.

"Sure, why not?" It was pretty good bourbon.

"Well, where was I?"

"Park Avenue, heart attack coming on."

"That's it. Felt it coming, he did. Well, being an educated man and all, he tried to get to a doctor, a lot of big society doctors in that part of town. So he goes into an apartment lobby, looking to see if a doctor is listed on the directory. Keeled right over dead, he did, trying to reach up to ring a doorbell. Well, there you have it."

15

"That's it?"

"That's it. Here's the report, all filled out and proper."

"The report makes it official, I guess."

"Official enough. A touch more bourbon?"

"No, really, I'm fine. Who found him?"

"A couple of sector cops riding by saw him; good boys they are, but he was gone when they got to him."

"No 911 call?" I asked.

"Nope. Now here's the Admiral's briefcase, still locked and sealed, and his wallet. Nice pictures of his family, a sad thing indeed."

Sullivan continued, "I know the drill. I'm an old Navy man myself. By the way, what's this lieutenant commander business? I thought all you Naval Investigative people were civilian civil service."

"Yeah, for the most part. I was commissioned out of the N.R.O.T.C. program at Notre Dame and spent a lot of years on active duty, mostly with the old office of Naval Intelligence. But I got rolled back to the reserves and went over to the N.I.S."

"Notre Dame," Sullivan pronounced slowly, "not too shabby."

I looked at the photos in the wallet - wife, children, grandchildren - nice people.

"Now, if you would be good enough to sign for these things, we'll just close out the matter."

"Maybe I should talk to the officers who found him, you know, just for the record, just so there's no second guessing later on."

"Yeah, I see what you mean; too bad though. I sent those very fine officers home. They were on overtime as it was and it's always upsetting dealing with a dead body, even for policemen. More bourbon?"

"No really, no thanks. Well, maybe I'll just swing by tomorrow and chat with them. What were their names again?"

"Well now, Jake, I'd say that would be a good idea but shift change, they'll both be off for a few days."

"Oh, okay," I said agreeably. "What were their names again? Just for my report."

"Now, Jake, here's the thing of it; I myself signed off on the report so my name is all you'll be needing, isn't it." It was a statement, not a question.

"Where's the late Admiral now?" I asked.

"Down at the morgue, along with the rest of his personal effects."

Sullivan stood up, signaling that the meeting had ended. I got up and signed for the Admiral's belongings, took my copies of the NYPD reports and thanked Sullivan for his efficiency and hospitality. On the way out the door, I turned and asked one last question.

"Captain, are you sure I shouldn't talk to the two officers?"

"I'm sure, very sure. But look, if you have to, I think you'll find apartment 812, at the address in the report, well, let's just say interesting. But remember Pandora's box, and our report tells how it happened. Goodnight, Mr. O'Brien."

I was glad to get outside and into my car. I lit a cigarette and turned on the radio; "Sunset Grill" was playing. I had to get the Navy's machinery in gear to notify next of kin - those nice people in the wallet, all of whom were sleeping peacefully someplace right now. That meant a trip to the morgue. I headed south on Park.

The only pedestrians between 33rd and 23rd Streets were the late-shift hookers. Tall, short, fat, thin, black, white, Oriental, Spanish, in every type of costume. A supermarket of exotic and sleazy sex. An interesting slice of New York City night life. Ironically, some gave a friendly wave to my car, glad to see what they assumed was a police car. At this hour there were a lot of weirdos and creeps on the street. But the truth of the matter was that we were, in a sense, related. We were all people of the

17

night.

Twenty minutes later, I pulled up in front of the Medical Examiner's office, which housed the City's main morgue. Police cars, ambulances, hearses, fire trucks and other vehicles littered the street around the huge Gothic building which took up a full three blocks beginning on the corner of East 30th and 1st Avenue. The rest of the street was dark and deserted but the Medical Examiner's building was lit, with all manner of people coming and going. I suspected ghouls lurked in the shadows.

The omnipresent smell of blood hung in the still lobby air. Experienced visitors ignored it, pretending not to notice it. First time visitors could be spotted by how the smell obviously assaulted them as they tried to figure out what it was.

I was a young Navy Ensign, very full of myself and right out of college, when I experienced the hot, pungent, sticky smell of blood for the first time. I had been sleeping on the floor behind the bar in the New York Club on TuDo Street in Saigon. That night, so many years ago, the Viet Cong detonated a recovered 500-pound iron gravity bomb in the alley next to the building. There was chaos, bodies everywhere and the smell of cordite and blood in the air.

Consulting the computer information console in the lobby, I figured out the room I wanted. I walked in and saw a short, fat, bald attendant with his shirt sleeves rolled up, displaying a collection of poorly done tattoos. He was attacking a Blimpie sandwich. He looked up from the Blimpie long enough to greet me.

"You need something?" he asked.

"O'Brien, Naval Investigative Service." I waved my ID past him as I spoke.

"Ya want to see the Navy guy they brought in a couple of hours ago? Nice uniform; he's dead."

Not knowing quite how to respond to that statement, I simply said, "Need to ID the body."

18

"Sure, he's dead as dead can be." With that, I followed the attendant into the room next door. The walls were lined with large filing cabinet-type drawers. Sandwich still in hand, the attendant selected a drawer and pulled it open. There lay the emaciated, naked body of a young, black, female heroin addict, so much for the glamour of the streets.

"Oops, wrong one; that's the OD that came in a little while ago. Here we go," said the attendant, as another drawer was pulled out, displaying the equally naked body of a white male in his mid-sixties, in reasonably fit condition, who showed the first glance signs of cardiac arrest. I made the identification from the Service Identification card in the wallet. My concentration was broken by the attendant saying, "Uh, uh, uh, no peeking."

The attendant pushed closed a slightly open eye lid on the body. With that, he broke out into laughter at his own joke.

I turned and left, leaving the attendant standing, eating his Blimpie and staring down at the recently deceased Admiral.

****

By 11:30 A.M., I'd gotten a couple of hours sleep, a shower, changed into a suit and picked up my partner, Mike Rossi. We drove up to 1150 Park Avenue, the address on Captain Sullivan's report. We walked past the All Visitors Must Be Announced sign, the door man and the concierge, both of whom began to stop us, but thought better of it. We took the elevator to the 9th floor, walked down one flight, and rang the bell on apartment 812.

After a moment, the door swung open and there stood a tall, blond, 30 year old woman with, as they say, a drop dead gorgeous body, which the short terry cloth bath robe did little to conceal. It looked like she had had a rough night. Then again, it looked like most nights were pretty rough for her.

"Wadda youse guys want?" Something about her voice

erased any doubts about her membership in the oldest profession.

"My name is Jake O'Brien; this is my partner, Mike Rossi," I said, holding my Naval ID, complete with anchor, in front of her face.

"Police," she responded, "well, I've been expecting you. You're here about the General, right?"

"Right," Mike and I said in unison. Our ID could have said *Intergalactic Space Patrol*, but to this lady, cops were cops, and General or Admiral were mere details.

"Well, for Pete's sake, get in here. I can't have coppers standing around in the hall. A girl's gotta watch out for her reputation, you know."

'Well, now, she deals with reality well,' I thought, as we stepped into the apartment and she closed the door behind us. No sooner were we in, when the blonde thrust an envelope into Mike's hand.

"Look, this isn't the monthly payment, it's something extra, a bonus. Yeah, that's it, a bonus for taking care of last night."

I grabbed the envelope from Mike, who had already started to put it in his pocket, and handed it back, saying, "I think you've got the wrong guys."

"Shit, you guys aren't from the Precinct?" a note of panic entering her voice.

"No, we're from the Navy," I said.

"Sam was a General in the Navy," the blonde stated, incredulously.

"Well, something like that," Mike offered.

"He was not," she paused. "I bet, oh damn, guys never tell you the truth; well, he was always a gentleman with me anyway, whatever he was."

I was wondering about her definition of gentleman when I caught Mike's eye; we were wandering off the subject.

"Look," I said, "someone will be around for the envelope,

probably a Captain Sullivan from Homicide."

"Homicide, Homicide, now just wait a minute. That's murder, isn't it?"

"It could be. Is that what happened?" Mike asked.

"Oh no, no, not at all," the blonde stammered, putting her hand on a credenza to steady herself. "Wow, I need to sit down. No, I need a drink."

'Decisions, decisions,' I thought.

"Look, guys, sit down. Can I get you something?"

"No, it's too early or too late or something," I answered.

"Speak for yourself, Jake; I'll have what you're having," Mike said.

"Okay, what the heck, make it three." I wondered what she, and therefore we, were having.

We sat on a couch. The blonde disappeared for a moment and came back with three water glasses half filled with gin and a solitary ice cube. She sat down opposite us and lit a cigarette, inhaling deeply.

"Thanks for the ice," I said.

"Too much?"

"No, just right." It was good I was retiring in a few months, my liver couldn't take much more.

"By the way, what's your name?" Mike asked, lifting his glass.

"Françoise LaTrec. Hey, you didn't know that?"

"Sure he did, just forgot, didn't you Mike?"

"Yeah, slipped my mind. Françoise LaTrec, nice name," Mike said with a note of sarcasm. I was tempted to add, "Had it long?" but refrained. She seemed pleased at what she perceived to be a compliment.

"I guess you guys want to talk about what happened to Sam. I'm not going to get in trouble or anything am I?"

"No, why should you? That's what you pay every month for, isn't it?" I said.

"You got that right, my dues." Boy, Françoise really had some strange definitions.

"Well," Françoise began, "Sam called yesterday and said he was going to be in town and wanted some company."

'Company he could have gotten at the Officer's Club,' I thought. "Did you keep him company often?" I asked.

"From time to time. I'd always fit him in, he was so generous and, well, he also sent a lot of his friends to me to arrange dates for them."

'Dates.' Françoise had such a way with words.

"So, he came up last night. About what time did he get here?" Mike asked.

"About 10:00 P.M. P.M., that's night, isn't it?"

"Right. Was he alone?"

"No, he was here with me."

"No, no," I said, "I mean, did he come here alone?"

"Sure. I don't do group stuff; what do you think I am?"

"Any more gin?" Mike asked, changing the subject.

"Sure, on the kitchen table. Better bring the bottle," Françoise suggested. In a moment, Mike was back, topping off everyone's glass.

"Go on Françoise, you're doing great," I said.

"Well, Sam and I were, we were, you know, we were..."

"Doing it," Mike contributed.

"That's it, we were doing it. Sam did it real good." Françoise continued, "Well, just as he, as he, as he..."

"Ejaculated," suggested Mike.

"Watch your mouth," Françoise shot back. "I told you, Sam was a gentleman and I don't do that weird shit; I got class."

"I know. Mike was joking," I said, trying to keep the flow going. "Let's just say Sam was about to...eh...stop doing it."

"Yeah, that's for sure. Sam did it and died."

Mike spit a mouthful of gin across the coffee table, somewhat spraying Françoise's terry cloth robe.

"Uck. Where did you get him from? He's no gentleman," Françoise yelped in disgust as she pulled back.

"No he's not; we all have our burdens to bear." I could just see the report now: "He did it and died and he did it real good."

"Just go on Ma'am; just give me the facts." She picked up at being called "Ma'am" and I was starting to feel like Joe Friday.

"Well, he died, just like that. Can you picture that? Dead, right on top of me. You know, my job isn't all fun and games."

"I imagine not! What happened then?" I asked.

"I rolled him off me, onto the floor. There he was naked, dead on the floor."

"What did you do then?" Mike asked.

"I got a drink."

Why was I not surprised?

"Then I came back and he was still dead."

"Really," I said.

"Yeah, still dead."

Maybe it was just me but this was the third person in the past 12 hours who seemed to have trouble with the finality of death in regards to the late Admiral Jeffries.

"Yeah, so I called the Precinct. I pay my dues, now I needed some help."

Generally curious, I asked, "Did the Precinct help?"

"Yeah, sure, a couple of uniforms came up. They should have sent guys in suits, like you two. Well, at first, they were going to call for an ambulance. I told them it was too late for that but they weren't listening to me. They changed their minds because of his medals and pictures."

"How's that, Ma'am?" Joe Friday speaking again.

"One cop kept saying, 'Look at all those ribbons; this guy was a real hero.' A regular John Wayne, the cop called him. The cop said something about the blue ribbon with white stars. I always liked that one."

It hit me. Of course I knew who Jeffries was. He was one of

23

the last surviving Naval officers to hold the Medal of Honor. 'Damn,' I thought, 'the Congressional Medal of Honor.'

Françoise was still talking. "The other cop was looking at the pictures in Sam's wallet and he was saying, 'Gee, what a nice family.' They said something about his pension, too. So they looked at each other and one guy says, 'What the heck?', and they get Sam dressed."

"Get him dressed," Mike started. "Was he still...?"

"Yeah, Mike." I cut him off before he could finish. "He was still dead." It must be something in the water.

"Of course he was still dead," Françoise said. "They," she repeated for emphasis, "they put his socks and shoes and everything on. Poor Sam. They even put his hat on him. Can you imagine that?"

At this point I could imagine just about anything.

"What happened next?" Mike asked anxiously, pouring himself another drink.

"They put Sam in the elevator and took him down to the lobby with his hat on." The late Admiral's hat seemed to have some great significance to Françoise; one could only wonder.

"Well, then one cop comes back upstairs, takes a look around, makes a phone call, tells me to keep my mouth shut and that everything will be all right, and he leaves."

"Speaking of leaving, we have to go," I said.

"That's it?" Françoise asked.

"Yup, that's it. What do you think Mike?"

"I think that's it, all right," Mike answered. "Say hello to Captain Sullivan when he stops by for the envelope."

"Sure, and thanks, I guess. By the way, how's Sam?" Françoise asked with great concern.

"Still dead!" I said.

We were walking down Park Avenue before Mike and I spoke to each other.

"Okay, how far do we take this?" Mike asked.

24

"What do you mean by that?" I responded, showing more than a little annoyance at the question.

"Look, the more we dig around, the more we find out, then the more we have to cover up."

Mike was right. While Françoise wasn't a mental giant, she did have her points and they didn't come cheap. Did the Admiral foot the bill or was it a defense contractor or maybe a lobbyist? What about the friends he sent up? No, this could get to be a real can of worms.

Mike broke into my thoughts by saying, "I say we go to lunch and forget the whole thing." Not waiting for my response, maybe trying to head it off, he said, "Look, Sporting Ladies and Navy Officers go back a long way, sort of a tradition, and you know how the Navy feels about tradition."

"Yeah, like Tailhook."

"That's my point exactly; they were amateurs, camp followers, not pros."

I thought how easy it is to rationalize support for a decision you've already made for other reasons. "How about The Dubliner's on Lexington? We can catch their Friday lunch special," I said.

"Sounds good to me," Mike answered. "What about the paper work?"

"Ah, give it to the secretary to file the standard forms using the NYPD report," I said.

"Sounds good. Going to the game tonight?" asked Mike.

CHAPTER TWO

January 12, 1904
Nevsky Prospekt
St. Petersburg

The Shpomka Banya was, in all likelihood, the most expensive bath house on Nevsky Avenue. The premium price was not for any additional luxury, save the all important one of discretion. It was for that they came - the Tsar's senior military officers, government ministers and shadowy men of influence. They came with their mistresses, common prostitutes and, on occasion, with their young male proteges.

Some sought out the group baths, some the private rooms; caviar, onions and imported champagne were consumed. Some indulged in the Russian obsession with pain, savoring the beating with reeds, claiming a throw-back to the traditions of the great Roman baths.

There was one at the Banya this night who was different. He was not one of the manicured, perfumed aristocrats but rather a filthy, disheveled Starets - the wandering peasant holy man who some were beginning to call a monk. Perhaps it was the repulsive appearance and manners that made him a menacing figure. More likely it was the devoted following he was acquiring in and around the Imperial Court. Whatever the reasons, he was accorded respectful treatment and given wide berth.

As usual, a private bath had been reserved for the monk. He sat on a stone bench on one side of the pool; mists of steam rose from the water. On the other side stood the woman and young girl.

The woman, in her mid-forties, was still very beautiful and prominently displayed on her décolleté a diamond pendant crest of the Romanov Family. Standing at a right angle to her and facing across the pool to the seated monk was a girl of no more than sixteen years. She was dressed in the finery of an aristocratic family.

The monk stood, drained a glass of vodka and threw the glass into the corner, where it shattered with the ring of fine crystal. He pulled his rough peasant caftan over his head, revealing his bony, scarred, filth-encrusted body.

The young girl cast her head down in embarrassment and revulsion.

Staring at her through the mist he spoke, "I do not pollute you but rather purify you." Without shifting his gaze he said to the woman, "Let her come to me."

With an expression of both pride and satisfaction, the woman slowly undressed the motionless girl, who began to tremble in fearful anticipation.

The last garment fell to the floor revealing a firm, round body with the developed figure of a woman but still showing the fleshy fullness of an adolescent.

The monk nodded in approval. He cocked his head and signaled with his hand to come.

The woman gently but firmly pushed the girl's shoulder. As if in a trance, she stumbled forward and descended into the pool, crossing to him.

****

27

Reborn and empowered through the sexual sacrifice of the young aristocrat, Rasputin left the banya and went to the Horse Guard's stable that he had had converted to his sanctuary. Climbing the stairs at the back of the building, he entered through the door reserved only for him. Then, proceeding through a series of doors inside the building, he appeared high above the chamber and took his elevated, throne-like seat in the east side of the cavernous room.

Beside the chairs, located at various points of the compass around the chamber, stood strangely clad men, each with a long, heavy, gold chain around his neck from which was suspended the emblem of his office in this secret lodge. All eyes were upon the master of the lodge, the great monk, Rasputin, believed by some to be the Messiah. With a flick of his wrist, Rasputin indicated that the candidate for admission be received for the initiation. After a strange and, at some points, frightening ritual, which included elements taken from Free-Masonry, the Rosicrucians, the Builders of the Atrium, and various Eastern occult ceremonial rites, the candidate knelt, blindfolded, before the altar.

One of officers of the lodge intoned the question, "In your present condition, what is it that you most desire?"

The candidate responded with the correct answer and by doing so saved his life. The answer from the candidate was, "Light." With that, the blindfold was torn away by one officer, while another jerked his head by the hair so that he could gaze upon the Light of the Lodge, Rasputin.

Rasputin was pleased, one more zealot to follow his mystical path. From these followers, and the twelve men of the Council which ruled the fraternity, Rasputin would secretly but effectively control all of Russia and, when Russia collapsed, as he knew it would, his Council would release his power like a virus throughout the rest of the world for years to come.

CHAPTER THREE

September 7
New York City

The Spring passed, turning to Summer and then to Fall. My papers were in and I was just waiting for my terminal leave date. In another couple of weeks I'd be a retired civilian. The thought of that gave me strange, mixed feelings.

All my cases and files had been closed or transferred. I spent my time now shuffling routine administrative papers, simply treading water. I amused myself by reviewing field investigators' expense reports - they were always good for a few chuckles. But the paper shuffling only contributed to my growing sense of uselessness. Maybe this demeaning holding pattern was bureaucracy's way of psychologically pushing you out the door. I had begun to have that anxious, all-I-want-to-do-is-finish-and-get-out-of-here feeling you get when you're still eating dinner at the only occupied table, ten minutes after the restaurant has closed.

I was even beginning to look forward to going upstate to the hamlet of New Paltz to sell antiques.

Suddenly, my secretary's voice come through the intercom. "A Mr. Thomas Jeffries to see you, Commander."

As I said, "Who?", a dapperly dressed young man strode

into my office, leaving the door open behind him. He leaned forward placing both arms on my desk and, taking control of the situation, declared, "I'm here for the truth!"

"Sure, you got it." I paused, "Truth about what?"

"What do you mean, 'About what?'; about my father, of course."

"Okay. So, who's your father?'

"You can drop that coy act. My father is, was, Sam Jeffries, Vice Admiral Samuel Jeffries."

'Good Lord,' I thought, as I saw my pension going right out the window. After two extended tours in Vietnam, a year in Lebanon, the invasion of Panama, several overseas covert assignments, and even a shootout stateside, just two weeks short of retirement, I could kiss it all good-bye. Life can really suck sometimes.

Memories of that night came flooding back - Captain Sullivan in his hand-made Hong Kong suit, the morgue attendant, and, of course, the unforgettable Françoise. Rallying myself, I stood up and said, "Okay, let's talk." I walked around the desk, closed the office door, and came back to sit on top of the desk. Young Jeffries sat down in the chair in front of, and below, me. Chess moves made; now I was in charge.

"You can start with the cover-up," he said, adding angrily, "Have you been drinking?"

Not knowing quite how to answer that I said with a mustered voice of authority, "Yes. Why yes, I have."

Being taken aback by my aggressive candor, he ignored the whole issue.

I continued, "What cover-up?"

'May as well brazen it through,' I thought.

"Look, let's get this straight," young Jeffries spit out as he leaned forward in his chair, stabbing his right index finger in my face. "My family is not without influence, I just graduated from Georgetown Law and have an appointment to Senator Dobson's office. So fool with me, and you, Mr. O'Brien, won't know what trouble is. So cut the crap and start talking."

That was it, pension or not, it was too late in my life to be pushed around by this little snot-nosed kid.

"Where would you like me to start?" I asked.

"The spies."

"The spies?" I replied. Boy, this guy was a real asshole, but maybe I was off the hook.

"Right. The Russian spies. I know the whole story. My father was killed, murdered by Russian agents because he was carrying classified documents in his briefcase. Those police reports are complete bullshit!" He was starting to whine.

"Well, you're right about the police reports."

"See, I was right. My father was a real hero and he died in action."

"Right again, on both counts."

"Then you're admitting that the police reports were falsified and there was a cover-up?"

"Sure was."

"Well, now we're getting somewhere. How did Dad die?"

I lit a cigarette, sucked the smoke in deep and blew it at the ceiling.

"Okay, I'll give it to you straight." I watched young Jeffries settle back into the chair, radiating satisfaction.

"Was it the Russians?"

"No, not exactly. Look, your father was a real hero. I read his 201 file. A real John Wayne, old school Navy all the way. So, let me put it to you this way, like John Wayne, he died in the saddle."

"In New York City?"

Boy, was this kid thick. "No, in apartment 812, with a..." Where was Mike when you needed him? "With a companion."

"You mean..?"

"Yeah, you got it. No Russians, just a broad named

Françoise."

"Oh no. How could he do it to Mom?" 'Good question,' I thought; 'truth was he probably wasn't.'

We talked a little more, but I don't think young Jeffries was really listening. Suddenly, he stood up and sort of shuffled out of my office, mumbling something about how could Dad do it.

I was lost in my thoughts until the secretary's voice came through the intercom again.

"Everything okay, Jake?" she gently asked.

"Yeah, I guess."

"Mike's on the net; wants to know if you want to meet for lunch at The Dubliner's."

"Yeah, why not?" I said, hearing the weariness in my own voice. I knew the time had come to get out.

****

Some days never seem to end. I turned off Pell Street and walked the block or so to Lu Chen's Chinese Restaurant; I had planned to get a bowl of soup or something before I turned in for the night. But there she was, big as life, smoking a cigarette and drinking a cup of tea. Chen tossed me an apologetic look from behind the counter as if it was his fault my ex-wife was laying in wait for me at his place.

"Tea, Boss?" he said.

"Yeah, Chen," I replied.

"Hot and Sour Soup?"

"Nah, I lost my appetite. Just the tea, Chen."

"Okay, Boss."

Chen set the tea down in front of me as I sat down on the stool next to JoAnne. "Out slumming tonight?"

"I wouldn't be," she said, "if you lived in a decent neighborhood."

"Come on. Chinatown is one of the great tourist attractions

32

of the Big Apple."

Maybe, if you lived on Mott or Canal Street. But back here, in this warren of alleys, it's like something out of an old Fu Manchu movie."

"Maybe that's why I like it down here."

"Don't start with 'my years in the Navy in the Orient.'"

"Okay. How about- 'If you can't afford to live some place decent, you might as well live some place colorful?' So, what do you want?"

"I've got a list of things, Jake. Alimony, child support, college expenses for Rachel, your retirement, visitation, my trip to Europe..."

"Good God, isn't this why we got divorced? You've got more things to discuss than the U.N."

"For Pete's sake, Jake, that's the trouble with you. You never could talk about anything seriously. You avoid responsibility, you change the subject, you just want to insult and argue. I want to do something with my life and you're content to live in a hovel over an ethnic restaurant in some off-beat, run-down neighborhood."

She was standing up now and shouting. None of the patrons seemed to notice. She threw her cigarette on the floor and crushed it out with her foot and, with the pronouncement, "I'm leaving," she slammed through the door and up the three steps to the sidewalk and disappeared into the night.

"Hot and Sour Soup now, Boss?"

"Okay, Chen."

"So much for wife," Chen said, laying down the soup, "how's daughter?"

"How should I know?"

"Chen been married five time, many daughters. All women crazy."

"How about an eggroll, Chen?"

CHAPTER FOUR

October 2
New Paltz, New York

The mountain was alive with color: reds, orange, yellow, browns sprinkled with an occasional dot of green. The Victorian porch of the New Paltz Antiques Center faced the side of Mount Mohonk, which had to be one of the most picturesque peaks of the Catskill Mountains. I had grown up in an old Dutch Colonial stone house on the opposite side of Mohonk. The house had been filled with an eclectic collection of serviceable antiques which had been passed down through the various generations of my family's ownership. Although I had seen a good part of the world, including a number of beautiful and exotic places, I felt no place more at home than in the gentle mountains that formed the Hudson Valley. As I stood there feeling the warm autumn sun, I was at peace with myself. The French Vanilla coffee from the cafe next door had come to replace my morning shot of Jack Daniels. It was hard to conceive that such a place of beauty, peace and tranquility was only seventy-some miles from the madness of Baghdad on the Hudson, also known as New York City.

My reverie was broken by the sound of footsteps on the porch. I turned to greet my first Monday morning customer. But life can really suck sometimes. The customer turned out to be my ex-wife's lawyer.

"Mr. O'Brien, how are you?"

"Counselor."

"It certainly is a beautiful day."

"Yeah, it certainly was."

"I must say you look well. Retirement must agree with you."

"I'd like to get back to the beautiful day, so what's on your mind?"

"Good, right to the point, Mr. O'Brien. I have some business to discuss with you. Mind if we sit here?"

"I'd rather go inside," I replied, not wanting to share my view with him.

"As you wish."

I led him into the main showroom and positioned myself behind the cash register. He stood on the other side, showing a little annoyance at being made to stand. He laid his briefcase on the counter.

"As you know, I represent your wife's interests in regards to your divorce."

"Ex-wife," I corrected.

"Quite."

"And it wasn't so interesting," I added.

Ignoring my comment, he continued. "I'm here to discuss your continued financial responsibility to JoAnne and your daughter, Rachel."

"Ever hear the expression, *You can't get blood out of a stone?*" I said.

"A turnip."

"A what?"

"A turnip, Mr. O'Brien, a turnip. I believe the expression is, *You can't get blood out of a turnip.*"

"Turnip, stone, whatever. You can't get blood out of either of them."

"In any case, Mr. O'Brien, as you well know, the courts have ordered that sixty percent of your pre-tax income goes directly to your wife and daughter plus, of course, medical and educational benefits." He paused, then continued. "While you were employed by the United States Navy, those funds were deducted directly from your pay."

"So that's it. I was wondering why I was the only guy who cashed his check at the subway station."

"Coming to the point, Mr. O'Brien, you are no longer employed by the Navy so payments to your wife have ceased."

"Right. So maybe she can marry that screen writer she's been shacking up with."

"It's a little inappropriate for jealousies at this point, Mr. O'Brien."

"I'm well over that emotion. I'm just a little tired of me working and her getting the money."

"You had a career with the Navy, one which she shared and supported during the years of your marriage."

"Is that what you call sleeping with half the enlisted men in the Sixth Fleet?"

"Really, Mr. O'Brien, I hardly think you've lived such a chaste life yourself and I believe that the basis of the marital breakdown was a consequence of your problems with alcohol abuse."

"Abuse? I have never been to an A.A. meeting in my life."

"How unfortunate. Look, the reason I traveled here was to have these papers signed," he paused while withdrawing a folder from his briefcase. "Your signature where indicated authorizes the same direct payments from your pension funds." He concluded by holding out a Bic pen.

'Jesus,' I thought, 'broke again.' I felt sick. I could refuse. I could fight it. I had fought a lot of battles in my life. But I wouldn't and the man with the Bic pen knew it. So I signed.

As he walked out the door, he turned and said, "By the way,

are you making any money here yet?"

I didn't answer and he knew enough not to push it.

As he went down the walk, he called over his shoulder, "I almost forgot - your daughter, Rachel, is coming for a visit tomorrow."

If I hadn't been so taken back by his last remark, I would have called out some smart-assed comment.

That's when I saw him, passing the lawyer and strolling up the walk. 'Ah,' I thought, 'my first customer.' He looked like a history professor from the local campus; brown oxford shoes, rumpled, nondescript slacks, an open shirt and corduroy jacket all screamed professor. Two 35 millimeter Nikons and one German-type camera all swung from his neck. Strange, but not out of keeping with some academics. Up the steps he came, extending his hand.

"Mr. O'Brien, Howie Littlepage here."

The thinning, slightly long brown hair connected to his not-so-trimmed beard. His smile was pleasant but the dark eyes betrayed him. This clearly was a man who could, if provoked, be dangerous. It was hard to tell his age and, looking closely, one could see the beard hid old scars.

"I'm O'Brien," I said, wondering what I did to make this day turn out so bad.

"Well, by way of introduction, we both share the same alma mater."

"Notre Dame?"

"No, the Navy. I did a stint a long time ago with the Office of Naval Intelligence then went over to the National Security Agency. Retired out of there on a disability. I work for a corporate security firm out of Connecticut now."

He handed me a card; it read *Intertell Systems, New Haven, Conn.*

"What can I do for you, Mr. Littlepage?" I asked suspiciously.

"Well, actually, I'm up here on my own; some old friends

asked me to free-lance something. Maybe we can get together a little later, after the shop closes, have a couple of drinks or something. Must be a good watering hole in town.

"What's the subject?" I asked.

"Sam Jeffries, Admiral Samuel Jeffries."

'Hell,' I thought, 'not him again.' "You wouldn't be working for his son by any chance?"

"No, I hear he's a real asshole."

"You got that right. Okay, I'll meet you at Foley's, down on Main Street about 5:30. I don't think I'll be able to help you but, sure, I'll tell you what I know." 'Maybe,' I added to myself.

"Thanks a lot. See ya then."

With that he turned and retraced his steps down the walk. I watched him get into a beat up Japanese pick-up. The left fender was crumpled and paint was flaking off the body. 'A real class act,' I thought.

Mondays in the shop were usually slow so, between customers, I intended to get on the phone and check out Mr. Littlepage. After all, I knew he was giving me the time to do just that. But my checking consisted of only one call, a call to my old office.

"Naval Investigative Service," answered an unfamiliar voice. A new receptionist, I thought.

I asked for my old secretary. "Let me speak to Sandra."

"I'm sorry, she's not in today."

"Is Mike Rossi around?"

"I'll transfer you, sir."

'Strange,' I thought.

After a slight delay I heard, "Public Affairs Office. May I help you?"

"Uh, no. I was looking for Accounting." I clicked the phone down. Public Affairs generally meant only one thing. I'd make the meeting with Littlepage for sure now.

When I walked into Foley's, the five o'clock happy hour

was well underway; the place was crowded and noisy. Both of us would be safe from the potential of the other recording our conversation. We were on neutral ground. I looked around and saw Howie Littlepage waving affably to me from the upper level. He sat at a corner table, back to the wall. Next to him, now wearing the ubiquitous three cameras, was an attractive young woman, perhaps a local graduate student.

I walked up to the table, "Mr. Littlepage."

"Mr. O'Brien." He drew out the name, making a formality into a friendly, familiar exchange. "This is Cindy, Cindy this is the gentleman I was telling you about. So, run along and give us a few minutes."

"Sure, Howie. Nice to meet you, Mr. O'Brien." Cindy slipped out of her seat and melted into the crowd, cameras clanking around her. I wasn't overly concerned as to what Littlepage had told her since it probably wasn't even close to the truth.

"What's with the cameras, Littlepage?" I asked.

"Into free-lance photography. Would leave them in my vehicle except the truck has no locks so I have to lug them around.

A waitress appeared as I took Cindy's seat. "A double Jack Daniels, on the rocks. What are you having?" I said, turning to Littlepage.

"Another club soda," came the reply.

The waitress disappeared. "A teetotaler?" I asked, thinking that was not a good sign.

"No, just a drunk on the wagon for a few years now. I'm one of those A.A. types, but not the obnoxious kind. And just to keep you from asking, the girl is a charming Ph.D. candidate who, for some inexplicable reason, has offered to let me crash on her couch tonight."

"What's the story with Mike Rossi? I called in today and asked for him and got Public Affairs."

"Local cops found his body in his car outside a bar in Little Falls, New Jersey, last night. He had been drinking and died of an apparent self-inflicted, single gun shot wound from his service revolver."

There was a long silence between us, at least it seemed long. I felt a deep depression start to envelop me. But I wasn't feeling shock or grief and that fact contributed to my depression. I told myself that it was because I had already suspected Mike was dead. But I knew, in truth, that the years of dealing in death and misery, and life itself, had blunted me.

The waitress brought my bourbon and I drank deeply and ordered another double.

"Rossi didn't kill himself."

"No, probably not, but that's what the reports will read, just like Admiral Jeffries died of a heart attack. Who was it said that history is a commonly agreed upon lie?"

"What's your interest in all this?" I asked.

"Sam Jeffries has a brother named David who's a big-time Washington lawyer. He contacted me with the right introductions and said he was concerned about the circumstances surrounding his brother's death. Oh, no suspicion of foul play or anything. Seems the Admiral had a real bad ticker and was living on borrowed time. But some things in the original NYPD reports looked....well, a little convenient. David Jeffries wanted to know the facts so he could do damage control, if necessary, to protect the family.

"And himself."

"And himself."

"What else?" I asked, knowing that there is always something else.

"Jeffries, the Admiral that is, was carrying some documents that in the wrong hands might be embarrassing. 'Embarrassing,' was all the brother said. I had the feeling he didn't really know himself what the documents might be."

"This sounds like an old Sherlock Holmes plot," I said. "What's the connection to Rossi?"

"I don't know. I got in touch with him the other day. He was real receptive to me. It was like he was expecting my call but was real nervous. Said a lot of shit was coming down. He wanted to meet in some bar in New York called The Dubliner's. I made the meet but he didn't. Then I reached out for the police lieutenant on the reports."

"A guy named Sullivan."

"Yeah, that's him. But he's on an extended leave of absence of some kind. It seems that everybody who had anything to do with the Jeffries affair is either going to ground or dead. That's why I came to see you."

"Did you come for information or to warn me?"

"A little of both, I guess. So what can you tell me?"

"Not much. As far as I know, Jeffries kicked off from heart failure. What was covered up was that he was with a high class hooker when it happened. It wasn't his first visit there, either."

"Ever take his friends up there?"

"Strange you should ask; as a matter of fact he did. But you know, other than the obvious, there really wasn't anything suspicious about what happened."

"You talked to the lady then?"

"Yeah, she was straight with us."

"How can you be so sure?"

"You'd have to meet her."

"I'd like to. Can you go with me and make the introduction? It's beginning to look like you may have a stake in this."

He didn't add what my stake might be exactly but there were several definite possibilities. "I don't know, maybe," I said.

"Well, here's what you have to do. I'm going to be spending the night so sleep on it and let me know in the morning. Is your shop open tomorrow?"

"No, it's closed Tuesdays. But I live in the apartment over the store." I had a feeling he knew both those facts already.

"Okay. I'll stop by your place, say around noon, and you can tell me what you want to do then. How's that?"

His wording made my answer a foregone conclusion. I said, "Yeah, okay."

As if by some pre-arranged signal, Ph.D. candidate Cindy reappeared, cameras and all. She had a satisfied smile on her face as she opened the small purse that also hung from her neck. With a wink, she half pulled the proverbial nickel bag of marijuana out for display and approval.

"Well okay, Jake, have to be moving along. See you in the A.M." With that, Littlepage stood up and pushed the bag back into the purse and, taking Cindy by the arm, departed through the crowd.

I was alone, very alone, and I decided to drink myself into oblivion. So off I went, up and down the bars and pubs of Main Street, New Paltz, feeling very desolate and out of place. When I knew that I was within a few minutes of passing out, I walked out of some bar and, with a feeling of relief, started the trek back up Main Street. I was proud of the discipline it took to stay erect and put one foot ahead of the other. I was doing pretty good but nonetheless, a town police car slowed up and looked me over before speeding away.

I made it to the Antiques Center and was tempted to stop and nap on the porch but kept going, up to the third floor apartment.

I fell back onto my bed. The room started to spin; I dropped one foot to the floor to stop the spinning. Then oblivion.

CHAPTER FIVE

October 3
New Paltz

I had been lying semi-awake for about an hour or so, allowing myself to drift in and out of sleep, attempting to escape the brutal hangover. Nauseousness, splitting headache, dizziness, extreme fatigue, were the worst of the physical effects of my self-inflicted wound. Beyond the physical discomfort however, was the depression, loss of self esteem and hopelessness that comes after a serious drinking bout.

I was trying to reconstruct the previous evening's events when the banging on the door downstairs began. I remembered this guy Littlepage was coming over. I staggered down the two flights of stairs, preparing myself to tell him to flake off. I reached the front door and, opening it, was assaulted by about a million candle watts of sunlight. Through the blinding light, I saw the silhouettes of two figures. One spoke.

"Hello, Dad."

"Rachel."

"Jake," said a firm voice, "do you mind if I come in?" Without waiting for a reply, he stepped out of the sun and into the house. "Rachel, dear, why don't you stay out on the porch while your father and I have a chat?" Again without waiting for a reply, he closed the door. It was Frank Dunlop, the screen-writing, live-in friend of my former wife.

"I see you haven't changed, Jake."

"I see you haven't, either," I said, steadying myself on a display counter.

"You were expecting us, weren't you?"

"Yeah, sure. It's just that..."

"I know, I know, Jake. You really should get some help but what you do with your life is your business. But, well, JoAnne and I want you to know that I'm very fond of Rachel and I have had some real concerns about having her visit you while we go to Europe. Seeing you now in this condition, there certainly is a basis for my concern - it looks, and I must say smells, like you slept in your clothes."

"I did." I wanted to say something like this was a mistake and I really wasn't drinking that much any more, but what was the use?

"Well," he said, "I'll take Rachel for 'coffee and..' in town, while you clean yourself up. I hear that New Paltz is the Greenwich Village of the Catskills. Say, an hour or so? Right. Then I'll be on my way." With that, he walked out the door and back into the million candle watts of light.

"Bye, Rachel," I called down the steps.

"Bye, Dad."

'SHIT. SHIT. SHIT.' Now began the ritual of getting myself together. Back upstairs I got a buttered bagel down followed by a handful of aspirins, antacids, a lot of vitamin B with a kicker of a few multis, and a bottle of GatorAde. Then shave, brush my teeth, mouthwash, a long, hot shower followed by clean clothes and back to the porch with a cup of coffee and dark glasses. I was ready.

But not for Howie Littlepage, who was coming up the walk smoking an ornate pipe; one that hopefully was filled with tobacco.

"Mr. O'Brien. How the hell are you?" he called out in a friendly voice. As he got closer he added, "Actually, you look a heck of a lot better than I expected."

"You should have been here about forty-five minutes ago."

"I'm impressed and surprised. I didn't think you were going to go with me."

"I wasn't. I'm not. Well, I'm not sure right now."

"Indecision - one of the effects of Demon Rum."

"No, the effect of an unexpected visit from my seventeen year old daughter."

"Seventeen, a delicate age. Shouldn't she be in school or something?"

"No, graduated last June and she's taking a year off before college."

As we talked, Frank's white Porsche pulled up and I watched Rachel get out, pulling a huge duffel bag from the rear of the car. As Rachel closed the door with the back of her foot, Frank half-waved and took off in a cloud of dust and gravel as if his life depended on it. Maybe he thought it did. Rachel walked up the path carrying her over-sized bag, looking like a well-dressed orphan.

I hadn't seen my daughter in a while and she surprised me. She had grown taller and thinner. She almost had the figure of a grown woman, but not quite. Some of her movements showed the sophistication and sexuality of an adult but there was still some gawkiness of a child. Maybe I was prejudiced but to me she was very pretty.

"Hi, Dad. Who's your friend?"

"Hi, Rachel." But before I could say anything else, Howie introduced himself.

"Howie, Howie Littlepage, and you must be Rachel. Jake's told me so much about you. You're just in time."

'Boy, was this guy full of shit,' I thought.

"In time for what?" she said haltingly.

"Yeah, in time for what?" I added.

"I know you don't think so, Jake, but she's old enough to come into the City with us. We can drop her off at a restaurant. Rachel can have a late lunch, we can make our appointment and pick her up on the way back. Okay. Well, we're all set." With that, Howie chucked Rachel's bag into the shop and, taking her by the arm, started down the walk.

"Hey, Howie, wait a minute," I called.

"Oh, Dad, I'm old enough to have lunch in the City by myself. Don't be such a dweeb!"

She turned back to Howie, "Howie - can I call you that?"

"Sure."

"Howie, can you drop me off at The Hard Rock Cafe? That place really rocks!"

"Why not? The manager is an old friend of mine. You coming, Jake?"

They were almost to the battered pick-up when Rachel realized that that was actually Howie's vehicle.

"We're going in that?"

"Sure, these trucks are really in when it comes to city driving, besides my other car's a bicycle."

"Oh," she said, looking somewhat perplexed. Events had exceeded my control so I acquiesced and squeezed myself into the back jump seat and dozed on and off during the 90 minute trip into the City.

Through the mists clouding my mind, I heard Howie telling Rachel how he was the son of a prominent Chicago lawyer, how they hadn't gotten along so he had run away from home as a young teenager and, with forged Seaman's papers, went to sea. After returning home and still having difficulties with his father, he left again, this time to join the Navy, and wound up in O.N.I. until his discharge when he was picked up by the National Security Agency, from which he was now retired.

Howie was clearly one of those guys who had a beguiling way about him. In appearance, he reminded me of an unkempt Amazing Randy. He was the type of guy that people instantly related to and liked. It was easy to see that he could get people to trust him. I had a sense he wouldn't betray that trust. Or maybe I was falling into a trap.

We crossed the George Washington Bridge and headed south on the West Side Highway, exiting onto Seventy-ninth Street, then heading cross-town to The Hard Rock Cafe. Making a wild U turn, Howie pulled up in front of the famous tourist spot and hopped out saying, "Come on, Jake, I want you to meet the Maitre d'; he's an old friend. Rachel, watch the car for a minute, will ya?"

I extricated myself from the back seat and walked towards the door with him.

"Howie, you don't know the Maitre d', do you?"

"Not yet but just follow my lead."

"Something I can do for you gentlemen?" said the beefy doorman who was looking past us to the beat up pick-up.

"Sure is," said Howie. As he spoke, he whipped out the gold shield of a 1st grade New York City Police Detective. "The manager in?"

"Right away, Officer. Anything wrong?" The doorman pushed a button signaling the manager.

"I'm Detective Faulkner, Public Morals Squad. This is Hank Williams from the State Liquor Authority."

A look of horror came over the doorman's face. The manager appeared.

The doorman said, "This is Detective...what did you say your name was?"

"Faulkner, like the writer." Howie began to look annoyed.

"Well, Detective Faulkner here is from Public Morals; this other gentleman is from the S.L.A."

Again came the question, this time from the manager, "Anything wrong gentlemen? Won't you come inside; to my office, maybe?"

"No. No time, " Howie said, looking at his watch. "We're pulling the liquor license," and, after a pregnant pause, he added, "of a place around the corner. You know the place."

"Oh yeah, sure," answered the manager, the color coming back to his face. "That real sleazy place, you know the one," he continued, turning to the doorman.

"Yeah, that one. Yeah, sure, sure," added the doorman, who seemed equally relieved.

"Look, here's how you can help. We've got a minor in our surveillance vehicle over there. Used her to make controlled buys but don't want her around for the raid. So would it be a problem if she stayed here for an hour or two?"

"No, no, not at all. Send her right in."

"Her name's Rachel, actually an innocent young thing."

"No fears, Detective." The manager was on his way over to the pick-up, signaling Rachel to come. In a flash, she was next to him and on her way into the club.

"Take care of her," Howie said to the doorman as he walked back to the pick-up.

"No problem, Detective."

"You do that kind of thing often?" I asked, as we walked back to the pick-up.

"No, I usually use the shield as a bathroom pass," Howie said, getting into the truck. "You know how few public bathrooms there are in New York; the tin gets me into employee bathrooms everywhere."

We drove over to the 1100 block of Park Avenue. I had a sense of deja vu as we passed the same doorman and concierge, again without stopping, and made the trip to the apartment of Françoise LaTrec. We rang the bell of apartment 812 and then knocked on the door. It was mid-afternoon so we figured she should be home. But no answer. So we tried the door and it opened. After a moment we stepped inside.

"Anyone here?" I called.

"Hi, honey, I'm home," called out Howie. There was no answer but the apartment had the feel of someone being there. We moved cautiously into the living room where Mike and I had sat and shared Françoise's gin.

There sat Françoise on a low foot-stool in front of the couch. She was naked except for the same terry cloth bathrobe she had worn during my previous visit. The robe, which was dotted with blood, had fallen open, exposing the large, firm peaks of her breasts. A cut showed below her left nipple. She was slumped over, staring at the floor and, without looking up, said in a child-like voice, "He's in the bedroom. He's dead. I killed him."

The air was thick with the smell of cigarettes from her chain smoking. Howie and I looked at each other and glanced around the apartment before entering the bedroom.

There on the floor he laid, spread-eagled, on his back, near the foot of the bed. Two small, neat holes dotted his forehead, his eyes wide open. An almost perfectly round pool of blood lay on the white carpet like a gigantic halo beneath his head. The dead man looked like a three-dimensional, life-size icon. His pants, and again the white carpet, were wet with urine. On the floor lay a pistol.

"God, this broad collects bodies like some guys collect base-ball cards," I thought aloud.

"I don't think this is going to fly as rough sex," commented Howie.

"Get a load of the gun," I said, "a High Standard .22 automatic, complete with silencer."

"Yeah, a real assassin's weapon. I haven't seen one of them since the Phoenix Project. The little lady is some shot. It reminds me of Kurt Vonnegut's book, *Dead-Eye Dick*," added Howie.

"Hot shit," he continued as he untied a legal size pocket folder on the bed. "Wow, there must be twenty or thirty thousand dollars here in American Express checks. Unsigned traveler's checks," he added

"You wanna call this in?" I asked.

"We better get some answers first. Why don't you take a look around? I'll check on the broad."

About ten feet from the body, high up on the bedroom wall, were blood splatters. Did that mean a second victim? This thing was getting out of hand. Howie zapped some stale coffee in the microwave and had given it to Françoise, who interestingly enough was stone cold sober. With great gentleness he was dabbing peroxide on the wound on her breast. He seemed oblivious to her nakedness and looked like a father treating a child's wounded knee. He finished and Françoise pulled her robe closed and sipped the coffee.

"Well, it looks like you had some problems here," Howie said quietly.

"You're the guys from the Navy. I don't remember you too good but I remember him," she said, nodding in my direction.

"Mike couldn't make it today, so Howie here came to help out. We and the boys from the precinct took care of everything last time and we will now. But you'll have to tell us what happened so we can take care of things."

"Yeah, after Sam died. But this is different, I killed him."

"Was there someone else here, too?" I asked.

"Yeah, I shot him, too."

Howie and I exchanged glances. 'Christ,' I thought, 'this is getting nuts.'

"Let's start at the beginning," Howie said, lighting a cigarette for her. "What time did they come?"

"I don't know. I don't know how long I've been sitting here."

"I think it's been a few hours," Howie said. "Just tell us what happened."

"Well, this guy called up and said he was a friend of Sam's and that he and his buddy wanted some company. Could he come over and maybe I could arrange a date for his friend. He said money didn't matter. His friend, he said, was loaded. They wanted to do dinner and a show, the whole works - all night, you know.

"So you let them up."

"Yeah, as soon as they get in one guy pulled a knife."

"The guy in there."

"No, the other guy." Françoise drank down half of the cup of coffee and took a deep drag on her cigarette then stubbed it out.

She was coming out of her shock-like state. Talking about it seemed to be helping her.

"Go on, Françoise," I said.

"Well, he made me sit on the couch while the other guy looked around; then the other guy asked me for the papers Sam kept here. I don't know how he knew about the checks."

"Besides the checks, did Sam keep other papers here?" asked Howie.

"No, just those unsigned traveler's checks and the numbers that go with them."

"What numbers?" Howie asked.

"The numbers on the papers in the bag with the checks. They had something to do with cashing the checks but I couldn't figure them out."

"Did you ever try?" I asked. Howie went into the bedroom and returned with the folder. He pulled out several sheets of paper and handed them to me.

"I never touched Sam's things until after he was gone. I figured it would be okay then but I was afraid of cashing those checks. I counted them. I counted them a lot. It was fun, like Monopoly money. There's $50,000 in there."

"Was the gun in there, too?" I asked.

"Yeah," she said, looking down at the floor. I had to do it; they were going to kill me. I knew they wanted the checks. At first I said I didn't know what they were talking about. That's when he cut me."

"On the breast?" Howie asked gently.

"Yeah, they said they were," Françoise looked down and began to cry, "they said they were going to cut my nipples off. Oh, God." Françoise dissolved in tears.

I held the rest of the coffee up to her and she finished the cup.

"I can deal with freaks but these guys weren't freaks. That's what made them so scary. Who are they?"

"Assassins, Françoise," Howie said softly. "Assassins."

"What did you say?" she asked.

"They were bad people, Françoise," he said.

"Tell us what happened then," I said.

"I knew they were going to kill me one way or the other and that Sam had that gun in the bag, so..."

"So, you got the bag, pulled the gun and shot them," Howie stated.

"Yeah, the other guy didn't die, he ran away."

"Françoise," I said, "listen to me carefully. These men were going to kill you but not for the checks. They wanted these papers."

"But they're just numbers."

"No, Françoise, it's a cipher, you know, a code. They, or whoever sent them, wanted the information on these papers."

"Are they going to come back?"

"You can count on that," Howie said.

Françoise jumped in her seat when the intercom buzzer gave off three long, loud blasts.

"What's that?" I asked, contemplating what might be coming next.

"The concierge's signal to warn me the police are on their

way up."

"I don't think that's the police," said Howie, with more than a note of concern in his voice.

"Françoise, listen to me. Where do you go to hide when the police come?" I asked.

"To the apartment across the hall."

"Do you have a key?"

"It's got one of those combination locks."

"Let's get out of here," Howie said.

"We're going, Françoise," I said, taking her by the arm, pulling her up and towards the door.

"I'm not dressed."

"Listen, Françoise, those men are coming back to do terrible things to you. We have to go NOW," Howie emphasized the last word and spoke with an authority I hadn't yet heard from him.

We crossed the hall, Françoise in tow, Howie carrying the file under his arm. She pushed the numbered buttons on the lock.

"Was it 356 or 635 or...?"

"Let's go, honey, get it right," Howie said.

I watched the numbers above the elevator at the end of the hall - 5,6,7, then 8 lit up. The elevator bell rang softly, I heard the lock snap open and we shoved Françoise through the door as my peripheral vision caught the elevator door start to open.

"Are you carrying, Howie?"

"No, I left my piece upstate."

"That does us a lot of good."

"Well, I don't see you bristling with fire power."

"I didn't know we were going to be an episode from *Murder She Wrote*."

"Will you guys stop it? I need some clothes."

Howie opened a closet by the door and pulled out a man's London Fog rain coat.

"This will have to do for now."

"Whose apartment is this, anyhow?" I asked.

"A girl who used to be in the life married an old lawyer or something. They're on a trip now."

"Is there a back way out of here?" Howie asked.

"Yeah, through the kitchen you can go to the basement in the service elevator."

"Sounds good to me," I said.

We took the elevator to the basement and crossed over to the service entrance. After pausing for a moment, Howie suddenly crashed through the door into an alley yelling, "Cover me," and slamming into the garbage cans as he went.

Françoise looked at me and said, "You don't have a gun, do you?"

"Ah, no I don't."

"What the hell are we supposed to do, piss on them?" she asked sarcastically.

Before I could think of an appropriate reply, Howie was back. "Okay, let's go," he said.

In a moment we were on the street and back at the pick-up. Françoise made the usual questioning comments about Howie's vehicle but agreed nonetheless to crawl into the jump seat.

Howie pulled out into traffic and Françoise spoke first.

"Don't you guys have a police car or something?"

"No. Why should we?" I asked, checking the rear view mirror to see if we were being followed.

"Aren't you arresting me?"

"What for?" Howie and I asked simultaneously.

"For murder, that's what for. I shot that man right in the head and now he's dead."

"We noticed," I said.

"Look," Howie interjected as he darted in and out of traffic, "absolute self defense. You defended yourself in your residence against two men who were in the process of committing a whole list of felony crimes. The Mayor will give you a medal. Besides, those guys weren't virgins."

"Sex had nothing to do with this," she said.

"Just an expression. He means that those guys probably had a long history of doing bad things like this."

"So I'm not going to go to jail?"

"Nope," I said.

"So, where are you taking me?"

"I don't know. Where are you taking her - us?"

"Let's go to ground upstate for a couple of days until we can sort this thing out."

"Okay. Listen Françoise, your friend, Admiral Jeffries, was into something, something real serious and you got left holding the bag, quite literally."

"The checks?"

"No, not the checks. I know that $50,000 seems like a lot of money but, well, to the government, it's not. You see, government agencies, a lot of times when they are doing something secret, they use unsigned traveler's checks to pay the expenses. You know, the CIA and NSA. That $50,000 was Jeffries emergency slush fund for whatever he was working on."

"And whatever that was is written in code in the numbers on those papers," Howie interjected, "and somebody, some group of people want to keep this all secret so badly that they have started killing anybody who they think has found out about it."

I was surprised at how simply we, particularly Howie, had summed up the whole situation, in one syllable words, or less.

"You guys are like spies, then."

"Something like that," I said, realizing our vague status was not quite so simply summed up.

"You're nice guys but I don't want to be involved in all this."

"That's the problem, you already are," commented Howie. "Self defense or not, you did shoot that guy, actually two guys; then there are the killers that are looking for you, and the government, at some point, is going to want to talk to you. Like it or not, you're involved," he ended with a chuckle. "But you're in luck - part of our job is to keep you safe and get you uninvolved. So here's what you've got to do. Oh, wait, here we are. We'll talk later at Jake's hideout."

'Great,' I thought as we pulled up in front of The Hard Rock Cafe, 'now I've got a hideout.'

"Look, Françoise," I said, " we didn't really expect today to turn out like this. My daughter is visiting with me. We dropped her here so she's coming with us and, well, I don't think she needs to know about any of this. We'll just say you're a friend or something."

"I got you. You might lose your visitation rights what with me and the guy back in my apartment and stuff."

"Very perceptive," Howie said. "Do you have any children?"

"No, but a lot of guys I date are divorced and have problems with custody and visitation and they talk to me about it. I'm sort of like a therapist."

A brief silence fell over the car as Howie and I contemplated that remark.

Suddenly, Howie jumped out of the truck saying he'd be back in a moment with Rachel, who was, when they returned, aglow to the point of being hyper. Surprisingly, without complaint, she squeezed into the rear seat already crowded with Françoise.

"Oh, Dad, what a time I had." Turning to Françoise, "Oh, you must be Françoise. I'm Rachel. I'm so sorry about your apartment. You must be so upset."

"My apartment...? I thought...," stammered Françoise.

"Howie told me all about it. Your whole apartment burned out and that you got out with just a bathrobe and slippers. But don't worry about a thing. We'll go to the mall and get you some new, neat stuff. Dad, there is a mall up by you, isn't there?"

"Of course, Rachel."

"Dad, can Françoise stay at your place?"

"Sure, you two girls can have the bedroom. I'll sleep on the couch."

"What kind of place does your dad have?" inquired Françoise.

"Dad calls it an antiques shop. Uncle Frank, that's the guy that sort of lives with my mom, calls it a sad forties shop."

I made a mental note to discuss that with Frank when next we met.

"How was your day, honey?" I asked.

"Great! Howie really made it happen. His friend, the manager, was so nice and everything was on the house."

I glanced over to Howie who pretended to be concentrating on traffic. I didn't know whether to be pleased or annoyed. I realized I was a little jealous.

"And guess what happened? Puck came in!"

"The Puck from *The Real World?*" interrupted Françoise.

"Yeah, cool! He's really a nice guy when you meet him in person."

Wanting to be part of the conversation, I asked, "Is *The Real World* a soap opera?"

"No, Dad," answered Rachel, sounding exasperated. "It's MTV. They select young people from around the country and put them in a loft apartment or some kind of neat house in cities like New York, San Francisco or London, and they have their lives videoed so you can see life in the real world. That's why they call it *The Real World.*"

"Yeah," Françoise added, "now they're sending them on vacations, too."

"Do these people work or something?" I asked.

"No," Françoise said, "MTV pays all their bills. Some of them get part-time jobs for fun or extra spending money but they don't need to work."

"And they call this the real world," I said, noticing that Howie had prudently elected to stay out of the conversation.

"Dad, you really should get out and see more of life and get with it." With that, Rachel and Françoise became lost in the discussion of lives of *The Real World* people.

Still feeling the effects of a serious hangover, I dozed most of the way back to New Paltz. Howie had said he wanted to stop by the apartment of Cindy the graduate student and pick up his cameras and things. I was pleased about that, particularly the things part. I was not pleased when he appeared back at the pick-up with the graduate student as well. To my amazement and the relief of the females in the back seat, she swung herself into the back of the truck, and sat on the spare tire. I soon learned that Howie had invited her to spend the night. My quiet bachelor's apartment had apparently now been turned into an ambulatory schizophrenic drop-in center. When the Chinese delivery man from the China Garden arrived, I asked if he, too, would like to stay but he, perhaps wisely, declined. He departed in ecstasy when Howie told him to keep the change from the $100 traveler's check.

After what seemed an eternity, the group drifted apart. Howie and Cindy, the graduate student, went downstairs to spend the night on a Victorian brass bed; soon, a faint smell of marijuana wafted up the stairs. Rachel and Françoise chattered and giggled in the bedroom. As I contemplated the relative maturity levels of Rachel and Françoise, I drifted off to the grateful darkness of sleep.

PART II

THE CLUB

"These, having not the Law, are a law unto themselves."

The Bible
New Testament
Romans II

CHAPTER SIX

October 4
The Council Chamber
New York City

The twelve club members sat in their usual places around the massive oak table in the chamber high above Fifth Avenue. But today was different, a thirteenth man sat uncomfortably at the end of the long table.

He was tempted to leave. These men who had ordered him to appear here were obviously mental cases. 'Weirdo cult members,' he thought. But it would be unwise to just walk out on them, for it was equally obvious that these were very powerful men. Men who took for granted having their own way. Men who were sensitive to the slightest offense or insult. He feared them; he, who in his life had killed many times, for many reasons, in many places. He, the professional assassin, feared these men.

His ambivalence about working for them ended when he was presented with a small suitcase. Opening it, he saw it was filled with money, cash, U.S. currency, some 10's and 20's but mostly 50's and 100's - all in used bills - a great deal of money.

The man at the head of the table spoke, "I trust that will be sufficient to cover your immediate expenses?"

"Yes, yes, quite satisfactory."

The man at the head of the table spoke again. "We," he said, "we are displeased with the messy business at the whore's apartment."

"It was not my fault. What she did was not to be expected."

"We are not interested in fault," interrupted the man at the head of the table. "But we are expecting you to control things in the future. We will overlook this one mistake."

The assassin felt twelve sets of eyes boring into him.

The speaker continued, "Where is the whore now?"

"I don't know. She can't be far. People like that can't hide. We, I, will find her."

"Where is the private detective hired by the Admiral's brother?"

"I don't know. He hasn't been to his office in the past couple of days; I am having it watched."

"And the retired Naval Investigator, have you found him?"

"Yes, yes, I have," answered the assassin, thankful of finally being able to answer in the affirmative. He added, "He runs a shop of some kind in a college town upstate."

"Will he cooperate?"

"Doubtfully; he's kind of an eccentric and probably not given to either threats or bribery."

"Blackmail?"

"Unlikely."

"Family, a lover, something he values? Find that thing and take it away. Then we can exchange it for what we need."

"I hear he has a daughter someplace."

"That may be your key. But be advised, if you take the girl, we do not want her harmed or molested in any way. We are not that kind of people. Unless, of course, if she becomes a problem, then do not hesitate to eliminate her."

CHAPTER SEVEN

October 4
New Paltz

The morning sunlight flooded into the east dormer and gently drew me from an amazingly peaceful sleep. I thought about how good you feel the day after a bad hangover and, feeling generally good about myself, I washed up and put on some coffee. The activity brought Howie up from the second floor.

"Good morning, my friend," he said with an imitation Irish brogue.

"Have some coffee," I replied, feeling the rising annoyance in me for his intrusion into my morning contemplations.

"So I will. Nectar of the gods." After pouring himself a cup, he popped a pill into his mouth.

I had to ask. "Vitamins," I said?

"Prozac," he replied.

I heard an involuntary, "Oh" come from my mouth. Before I could comment further, I became aware of Rachel standing in the bedroom doorway.

"Hi, Dad, what's for breakfast?"

"I don't know. What would you like?"

Howie interjected, "I make great omelets." The three of us exchanged glances.

Howie broke the short but cold silence. "On second thought, why don't you make your daughter breakfast? I have to get Cindy back to her place." After a pause, he added, "And I want to put a call into D.C. and talk to my client."

"Good idea," I said, picking up a frying pan.

"How 'bout pancakes?"

"Ah, never mind, Dad. I'll just have some coffee later," she answered as she retreated back into the darkness of the bedroom.

****

It was about 10 A.M. when Howie causally strolled through the door of the Antiques Center.

"Nice of you to drop in," I said with as much sarcasm as I could muster.

"Yeah, yeah," he said slowly as if about to make some great pronouncement.

Not hearing one, I continued, "Look, Howie, we need to talk."

"That we do," he replied. Then turning away from me, he called to a Yuppy couple in the next room who were studiously examining a McCoy vase, "Go on, take it; you know you want it."

"But it's got a chip in it," they replied in unison.

"Gives it more character," Howie declared.

An incredulous look passed over the faces of the couple. "I guess," the woman replied. "We'll think about it," the man added. With that they replaced the vase on the shelf and left the shop.

"For crying out loud, Howie, I'm trying to make a living here."

"Yeah, well, that's why I'm here this morning. I've got a plan."

'This should be good,' I thought to myself.

"Look, Jake, what's your weekly take here. I mean the gross sales, not profit. Two grand?"

"Not hardly."

"Doesn't matter. Here's what you've got to do. I'll hire you for a week as a consultant. Put up an *On Vacation* sign, hang with me for a week. We wrap up this Admiral mess and all get on with our lives. I'll double your weekly take and then some. Say $5,000 for the week."

"Five thousand dollars! What are you, some kind of nut?" Remembering the Prozac, I realized that the question was probably rhetorical.

"No, just welcoming you to the club. Everybody retires from the Government and then makes a killing as some kind of consultant - now it's your turn." With that he pulled an envelope from his pocket and tossed it on the counter. It contained unsigned travelers checks.

"Ah, Howie," I said, hearing the disappointment in my own voice. "These are some of the checks we picked up yesterday."

"So?"

"So, they belong to the Government."

"The Government doesn't seem to be missing them."

"Oh, I see, you can steal as long as the victim doesn't realize that they're a victim. Boy you really take that philosophy quite a ways."

"The way I see it," Howie said, "is that Admiral Jeffries was going to use them to resolve whatever this whole thing is about. He's dead and we're taking over and are using the resources he left behind. Besides, what are you going to do, mail them back to the Pentagon?"

"That's not such a bad idea."

"Great. The Defense Department can use the fifty grand to buy two hammers and a screwdriver."

He had a point. I heard footsteps coming up the front porch; so did Howie. He moved to the front door, closing it somberly and intoning to the potential customers, "Sorry, closed. Death in the family." The couple turned and scurried away. Howie was really a weird looking guy sometimes. He put up the *Closed* sign and pulled the shade down.

I put the checks in my pocket.

I'm not sure why I went along with the plan. It seemed to be a fait accompli for a lot of reasons; maybe it was the money, maybe I was looking for a way to impress Rachel, maybe selling chipped vases hadn't turned out to be the Nirvana I thought it would be.

"Look," Howie said, "I talked to Lawyer Jeffries on the phone and brought him up to date. Not a happy camper."

"You tell him everything?"

"Yup. Checks, gun, body, ciphers, the whole enchilada."

"What was his reaction?"

"Upset, a little panicky. We meet him tonight at 7:00 at the Kingston Airport," Howie paused, then added, "Is that anywhere near here?"

"About 20 miles north. I hope he's coming in a small plane - it's not much of an airfield."

"That's his problem," Howie replied with more than a touch of cynicism. "Speaking of problems, any chance of figuring out what the number sequences on those cipher sheets might mean? By the way, where are the girls?"

It was as if Howie shifted gears in mid-thought. "They're upstairs, still asleep. About the coded material - you're the guy that used to work for NSA. I thought that NSA was the code-breaking outfit."

"Yeah, so they say, but I was a field grunt, I never got a decoder ring."

"I'm not surprised but you're in luck; your five grand buys you something worthwhile after all. There happens to be a retired code breaker who lives in the little hamlet of Rosendale, not far from here."

"No shit," Howie said, sounding truly amazed. "Where the hell's Rosendale?"

"Half-way between here and Kingston."

"No shit," Howie said with even more amazement in his voice.

We dropped Françoise and Rachel off at the Poughkeepsie Galleria Mall. Françoise had been temporarily outfitted in some vintage clothes from the shop. Surprisingly, she kind of liked the outfit. Howie provided them with a handful of travelers checks and, using his trusty New York City Police Detective's ID, arranged a plain-clothes security escort for them. With Rachel and Françoise occupied for the rest of the day and evening, we pressed on to Rosendale.

We came up Rt. 32, crossed the bridge over the old D & H Canal and turned left on to the main, and only, street of Rosendale. Driving the quarter-mile or so to the other end, we stopped in front of the Astoria Hotel. The Astoria was a four story structure with a bar on the 1st floor. It looked like it belonged on a set from *Gunsmoke*. No, it looked like it belonged on the long-abandoned set of *Gunsmoke*.

"Wow, this is a strange town," Howie said.

I wanted to answer something like, "Well, you sure qualify as a judge of strange," but simply stated, "Yeah, it's an old canal town that doesn't quite make it as a poor man's Woodstock."

As I started to get out of the pick-up Howie said, "Wait a minute. How come you just happen to know a code-breaker living right up the road out here in the sticks? An amazing twist of fate, perhaps, or just a coincidence?"

As usual my first impulse was to give a smart, one-line answer but I recognized his paranoia, paranoia that comes from never knowing the whole story, never being sure of anyone, always being sure that betrayal lies around the next corner. Accept something as coincidence and you may be deceiving yourself. The mystery writers dramatically say, "Trust no one," which, in reality, turns out to be true. But the end product of living year after year in distrust is cynicism, disillusionment and, eventually, personal isolation from the rest of the world.

"Lighten up, Howie. This part of the Hudson Valley has a long historical relationship with the intelligence world going back to the Revolution. James Fenimore Cooper's book, *The Spy,* was based on a guy who lived down the road in Highland; the American Communist Party was founded up the road in Woodstock; up at the Mohonk Mountain House, back at the turn of the century, were the first international anti-war protests..."

"Nice history lesson," interrupted Howie.

"Look, let me put it to you this way, within a fifteen mile radius, there's West Point, the old Stewart Air Force Base, Camp Smith, and half a dozen smaller military installations. A lot of military and intelligence types retire out and stay here."

"Okay," Howie said with a lilt in his voice, as if to say, "That makes sense."

We walked up the stairs and knocked on the door of a second floor room. After a moment, the door opened, revealing a shabby bedroom with a sink in the corner.

In front of us stood Jeanette Quinlan, a still attractive woman in her late sixties or early seventies. She wore a vested shirt and clerical collar.

"Jake," she said, "Jake O'Brien. How are you? Do come in; I'm so happy to see you. And who's your friend?"

There was a hint of tears in her eyes. 'Another isolated person,' I thought.

"It's good to see you, too, Jeanette; this is Howie Littlepage."

"Littlepage, Littlepage, Howie Littlepage. Your name sounds familiar. Who are you?"

"Littlepage, Howie Littlepage," came his answer.

"No, I mean, well, you're in the trade, aren't you?" she said, dropping a heating coil into a teapot.

"Retired from the NSA, retired on a disability."

"Now I remember. You're the one who got nailed down in Chile during the Allendez thing. Had a pretty rough time of it as

I recall."

"You've got a good memory. Yeah, I was the original cell-without-number, prisoner-without-name. The beard covers the scars pretty well, doesn't it? But I was the lucky one."

"How's that," I asked?

"My partner was killed."

"Did they ever find the one who betrayed you?"

"About ten years later. The Agency's got a long memory and they take care of their own. Enough about me. Are you some kind of lady priest or something?"

"No," she said, handing out instant coffee in Styrofoam cups. "But I am an ordained minister in the Reformed Church in America, you know, the Dutch Reformed Church."

I doubted Howie could tell a Mormon from an Orthodox Jew.

Jeanette continued telling him how late in life she had earned a divinity degree and fought a chauvinistic system to finally fulfill her life-long dream of ordination.

"Do you have a church or something?" Howie asked with genuine interest.

"No, they let me be ordained but, well, having my own church, that's out of the question. So I work as a Chaplain here and there. Howie, I've known Jake since he was a little boy and he wouldn't be here if there wasn't something on his mind. What's up, Jake?" Her voice was gentle but authoritative.

"You know I retired from the Navy and took over a shop in New Paltz. Well, something cropped up from an old case and, well, I kind of got involved in something here."

"*Once in, never out,* was the old saying," Jeanette interjected somewhat philosophically. "How can I help you?"

"Well, we've got these sheets with numerical sequences; it's a cipher of some sort. Jake says you used to be a code breaker."

"Going back to '44 with the F.B.I., then later with the NSA but it's been a long time. I don't know."

"Maybe you could just take a look at it," Howie said, handing her the folded papers from his jacket pocket.

She took the documents gingerly, almost reluctantly. It might have been my imagination but it seemed that a sadness began to envelop her as she contemplated the papers. In an almost trance-like state, she pulled glasses from her vest pocket and slipped them on. Long moments passed in silence. I began to wonder if she had simply spaced out.

So I asked, "Do you want to know some background?"

"No. No. That won't do," Jeanette said without looking up. "My conclusions must be analytical, not led by subjectiveness." After a brief pause, she continued, "This is Russian, you know; well, not really. We used to see this in the '50's; we called it the Latvian Ladder. It works on a system of progressions..."

"I thought you said it was Russian," Howie commented.

"Well, it's late 1950's, Soviet Navy," Jeanette replied, still not looking up. "There were a lot of Latvian officers in the Soviet Navy and they were quite nationalistic and somewhat hostile towards Marxism." Jeanette looked up, finally, taking off her glasses as she lay down the cipher sheets. "All Naval transmissions were, of course, in the Russian language and used Soviet Naval codes but the Latvian officers would encrypt them using their own system. I think they did it just to stick it to the Russians."

"Then this is from the 1950's?" I asked.

"Maybe not. The encrypting system was simple but effective so, from time to time, it popped up someplace else."

"What's it say?" Howie asked.

"I don't know yet. I'm going to have to make a code wheel and find my Russian-English dictionary. I might have some preliminary information by this evening, a few words here and there."

"A few words here, a few words there and we'll put this thing together," Howie said with his usual optimism.

We finished the coffee, said our good-byes and left, agreeing to be in touch later by telephone. Getting back into Howie's pick-up, I felt the depression that comes with guilt. It wouldn't take much to drop in from time to time and visit, maybe even take her to lunch once in a while, not just come because I needed something. I promised myself to do better in the future. It was a promise I knew I wouldn't keep.

****

Howie and I didn't talk much on the half-hour or so trip to the air strip generously referred to as the Kingston Airport. I suspected he was lost in some Prozac-induced haze, having just taken his afternoon dosage. For myself, I felt like a bit of flotsam bouncing from wave cap to wave cap, pulled by currents and eddies beyond my control. It was not a comfortable feeling.

We turned off Route 32 onto Airport Road. When the macadam turned to gravel, Howie shot me an anxious look. We pulled up to, and paused for a moment at, the sign which read, "Kingston Airport - Flying Lessons, Charters, Sightseeing." In front of us was a single, narrow, blacktop runway. Grass was sprouting up through the cracks.

"Jake," he said, "I gotta tell you - I saw better airfields in Laos back in the 60's."

'I didn't pick it.' I felt like crying out, 'It's not my fault,' when he turned to me and raised an eyebrow. Maybe he wasn't blaming me for the airport, but I bet he was sure as hell critical of the part of the country I had chosen to live in.

Howie parked his battered pick-up in the shade of the sole hangar next to the strip. He laid in the cab to take a nap and I checked into the shack that housed the office and then killed some time roaming around inspecting the tied down, single engine planes that littered the grass around the runway. A Grumann crop-duster by-plane sat off to one side, some distance away. Its

71

nose pointed disdainfully towards the mundane week-end hobby ships.

Just as I began to wonder what I was doing here in the first place, the sky clouded over and turned the air around me into a fine mist. For some bizarre reason I thought about standing out in the rain but found myself wandering into the hangar. Not seeing any NO SMOKING signs, I stuck a cigarette between my lips and fumbled in my pockets for a match. Suddenly, a lit match appeared before my face.

"And here you are, Jake my friend, but I must warn you that smoking is quite bad for your health, particularly with so much petrol about," proclaimed Howie in his imitation Irish brogue. Maybe it was the phony accent, maybe I didn't like him sneaking up on me, maybe I just didn't like the whole set up but whatever it was, I had had it and I turned to let him know it but before I could, Howie intuitively cut me off with a question. "So, how come you signed on to work this case with me Jake?"

"The money?" I answered.

"Sure, that's part of it," Howie said, "but there's more to it than that. I suspect their whacking your ex-partner, Rossi, has something to do with it."

I took some offense at his choice of words but he was right. My relationship with Rossi had covered a couple of decades in an on-again, off-again, kind of way. We first met when I was attached to the Office of Naval Intelligence during my second tour in Vietnam. Rossi was an enlisted Navy Quartermaster at the huge Army-Navy complex of Camron Bay. Rossi had been working black market deals with U.S. government scrip. He got picked up in a sweep and was turned over to me by Treasury agents. 'Gumshoes from Washington,' I thought with some disgust. It had been my opinion that Rossi's big sin was in getting caught in a periodic crackdown of something everyone did. I'm not sure why, maybe it was the nature of the arbitrary and inconsistent crackdowns, maybe it was the inherently moral yet eminently practical personality of Rossi. Who knows? I decided to make the case "go south,"as they say, sparing Rossi at the least a Bad Conduct Discharge or possibly some serious time in Portsmouth Naval Prison.

Over the years our lives and careers criss-crossed like planets and moons in some bureaucratic galaxy. We were both stationed in New York in Naval Investigative Service when JoAnne finally threw me out with, as the saying goes, "nothing but a fine-tooth comb." More than a week later, it was Rossi who found me in the Bowery where I'd landed during the binge that started when the door slammed behind me. He not only took me in and cleaned me up but covered up my absence as well. I think we both understood that now we were "even." We weren't close friends, we were more like companions. Perhaps we had both lost the ability to have a friend in the ordinary sense. Nonetheless, between us there was a bond of loyalty and trust that was quite unique. And now, I just had to do what I thought was the right thing, even if I didn't clearly understand why.

The sound of a plane engine overhead pierced the fog surrounding my brain and drew me from my reverie. Simultaneously, a tiny loud speaker crackled the message: "Mr. O'Brien, your flight is arriving." Without a word but with what I assumed was a sudden, mutually held feeling of comradeship, we walked out into the drizzle and stared high above the end of the runway. Howie held up one hand, shielding his eyes from a non-existent sun. 'What a screwball,' I thought. A descending plane came into view.

"Holy shit, is he going to clear that bridge?" Howie exclaimed!

"I hope so," I answered somewhat calmly. "I never understood how they could have an airport approach adjacent to a major bridge across the Hudson. The plane came in fast, cleared the bridge, and dropped its flaps and landing gear. Seemingly against all odds, it touched down onto the runway, racing past us before turning and taxiing back to us.

"He's a hell of a pilot," Howie declared.

The Piper Arrow rolled to a stop about fifty feet from us. A trim-looking man in a Brooks Brothers suit and dark glasses hopped out of the door as it opened. Next came an older, grey-haired man in a rumpled seersucker jacket, followed by another Brooks Brothers ad. The threesome walked towards us with the two Brooks Brothers scanning from left to right like human radar screens. Not to be outdone, we walked towards them, Howie making the point to look from left to right. His torso was slanted forward in an unnatural, exaggerated way. If I gave him a cigar, I swear he could have doubled for a bearded Groucho Marx.

As we came into hand-shaking distance, the two Brooks Brothers moved off in opposite directions, covering us from different angles while still scanning the over-all area. The pilot emerged and began to inspect the plane. He appeared in his mid-60's, a little pudgy but solid, wearing aviator's dark glasses and a classic brown leather flight jacket. Even at a distance, the large gold ID bracelet on his left wrist was clearly evident, a trademark that identified him as a former Air America pilot, the CIA's private air force of the 1960's.

"Littlepage," Seersucker said, extending his hand to Howie and, after shaking, extended it to me announcing, "And you must be O'Brien." I shook hands wondering if this guy ever used first names.

"Jake, this is David Jeffries, Esquire, brother of the late Admiral Samuel Jeffries," announced Howie, as if he were the butler announcing arriving guests at a grand ball.

With equal formality, came Jeffries response, "Yes, Jake, if I may call you that, you were the Navy man who identified my brother's body. I understand that you run a used furniture store now."

"Antiques," I said.

"Quite," he answered. "In any case, thank you for coming."

74

Turning to Howie, "Down to business. What have you got, Littlepage?"

"Not much more than when we talked this morning, except we have the coded information being worked on by a very competent analyst and we plan to start the debriefing of the prostitute tonight. We have a couple of other irons in the fire as well," Howie concluded, sounding both very efficient and satisfied with himself. I thought to myself, 'A typical government report making nothing sound like a lot.'

"Good. It sounds like you're getting things under control. Jake, you're on the team, right? You're in this thing with us," the last comment more of a statement than a question.

"Sure he is," interjected Howie before I could respond.

Cynically I added, "Yeah, I guess I've accepted the King's shilling," feeling the weight of the fifty unsigned travelers checks in my jacket pocket.

"Excellent," Jeffries said, grabbing my shoulder with the experience of a seasoned politician, "and I see by that comment that you are a student of history and a bit of a philosopher as well."

Wanting to reverse the tide that I was being sucked into, I asserted myself by asking a question, one that I thought was rather significant. "Isn't there the small matter of a body in Françoise's apartment? Not to mention some blood on the wall, a gun..." But before I could finish my litany, Lawyer Jeffries jumped in.

"It's all been taken care of. The whole apartment has been sanitized and a new rug will be laid in the bedroom in a day or so."

"Who the hell are you, anyway?" I heard the words come out of my mouth before I even consciously thought them. In a momentary burst of anger, I wasn't sure if I was questioning his capability or his right to sanitize anything.

"I can be your..." Jeffries started to reply before being cut off by Howie.

"Dave," he interjected forcefully, "why don't you fill us in on whatever background you can give us so we move along and tie this thing up."

I recognized that if Howie wanted a career change, he'd make a good arbitrator.

The lawyer turned to Howie and began. "Okay," he said, showing the fatigue which underscored for the first time the stress he was experiencing. "Okay. My brother was getting ready for an overdue retirement. As to be expected, he was being approached by a number of corporations and foundations who wanted his name on their boards. I was handling the contracts and legal issues regarding that for him. He met with some European historical-type society based in New York which, as Sam put it, was offering fantastic money and benefits. The outfit was a little vague as to who they were and what they were about and he figured that it was a front for some intelligence agency. The Soviets aren't around any more so it had to be U.S. But if it was U.S., why not a straight approach? It wasn't like he was some college kid being recruited by the CIA or something. Anyway, Sam checks around Langley, etc., and comes up with a blank. Then comes the clincher, the reason they want Sam."

"This should be interesting," mused Howie.

"Yeah, look," lawyer Jeffries continued, "Sam was the type of officer that legends are made of. No, he was legend in his own right and he had the resume to match, but he was a wild man, a maverick, frankly, a problem sometimes."

"And problems don't get the C.N.O. slot," I said, the light beginning to dawn.

"That's right. Sam wanted to and let it be known that he thought he had the right to retire out as a four star and to sit in the office of the Chief of Naval Operations, at least for a while and, well, it wasn't in the cards and he was, quite candidly, bitter."

"And bitter guys get recruited by the bad guys."

"Exactly," the lawyer said. "But who were the bad guys?"

"So why not just notify some counter-intelligence agency?" Howie added.

"Who? The F.B.I.?" answered Jeffries, with some disdain. "Anyway, it wasn't my brother's style. He was going to, in his own words, 'bust it open,'."

"Your brother might have been a great man on the bridge of an aircraft carrier but the cloak and dagger world was," I paused to think for a moment, "a world more familiar to you, perhaps?"

"Perhaps."

"So what's the big deal? The Admiral's dead - let Langley know what's going on and get on with life," Howie said philosophically.

"Well I'm not sure how far into it Sam got in his attempt to "bust it open" so some day when the FBI stumbles into this or something, well, I don't want my family to be the sequel to *The Walker Family: Family of Spies* on the Sunday Night Movie."

"A spectre always waiting in the wings," quipped Howie.

Without acknowledging his comment, Jeffries continued, "Plus I have talked to people who are concerned what this group was about. Look, I've had funds transferred to your company's account in Hartford. In addition, you can make use of the $10,000 in travelers checks. If you need anything else just contact me. But gentlemen, we need results fast."

The meeting was over. The Brooks Brothers, Seersucker, and Gold Bracelet were back in the plane and speeding down the runway towards the Kingston-Rhinecliff Bridge, which they just cleared.

I turned to Howie, "Ten thousand in checks?"

"Details. Details."

****

Without much conversation, we crossed the river and headed south on Route 9 to pick up Rachel and Françoise at the mall. A few miles north of the mall, Howie broke the silence, "So, is Dave telling us the truth?"

"Yeah, as far as it goes, but you can bet he's holding back a lot."

"To be expected but are his hands clean?"

"Pull over," I said, indicating a parking lot with pay phones near the curb. "I want to call Jeanette."

"Okay. I should call in to my office, too."

After putting an amazing amount of quarters into the phone, I got through. "Jeanette,"

"Jake, is that you?"

"Yeah."

"Thank God. Prayers are answered. Where are you?"

"Just north of the mall in Dutchess County. What's wrong?"

"Look, I went past your place in New Paltz on my way to the University Library to use some of their dictionaries and they're all over your place."

"Who's all over my place?"

"I don't know but I spotted at least three or four surveillance teams and I think they're from different agencies. They weren't FBI types or local police, that's for sure. I think they were private, private but professional, and they were heavyweight." She was speaking very fast.

"What do you make of it?" I asked.

"I don't know but stay away from there. You need to go to ground. I don't know what you're into but my gut says stay out of New Paltz."

"Great," I muttered.

"Jake, I took the precaution, the liberty, of lining up a place you can stay."

"I didn't ask you to." I showed my anger - I was getting a little tired of everybody arranging things for me.

"Well go to the Holiday Inn, then."

"No, Jeanette, I'm sorry. It's just that things are a little out of control and I'm on my way to pick up Rachel and someone else."

"*Calm in crisis* is the old saying. No problem, there's plenty of room for all of you."

I wondered if after a certain birthday you got a license to use the old sayings.

Giving into the motherly tones, I asked, "So, what do you have for me?"

"Good," she sighed with relief, "a dear friend of mine has a Bed and Breakfast in, well just outside of, Woodstock. It's kind of hard to find his place so maybe you could meet him in Woodstock."

"Where in Woodstock?"

"Say across the street from the Tinker Street Cafe, about 10, 10:30, tonight?"

"Does he take travelers checks?"

"Don't worry about that. He's..., he's..., well, been in the business."

I was tempted to ask what business that might be but didn't. I hung up and got back into the truck with Howie.

"How did you make out?" It sounded like a rhetorical question.

"Jeanette said there are some anti-social types sitting on the shop in New Paltz."

"Not surprising. Same thing my secretary said. The office is heavily staked out, too. What now?" he asked.

"I thought you were running the show."

"Me? No way. You're the local consultant. That's what you get the big bucks for."

"Jeanette's lined up a place for us in Woodstock."

"Woodstock? Great! Let's get the girls."

****

We picked up Rachel and Françoise at the mall. Their security guard escort actually saluted as we pulled away. For the first time, I appreciated the pick-up truck - it accommodated the assortment of bags and boxes containing their purchases.

The girls were exuberant from their day of shopping and the prospect of a vacation in a Woodstock B & B. I was beginning to hear phrases like, "Dad, you're the greatest." Howie was equally pleased about a sojourn in Woodstock. The basis of his exuberance both mystified and concerned me.

****

We pulled up across from the cafe on Tinker Street about 10:15. I sent the girls out to window-shop the stores that lined the street. It didn't take long before he came.

"This looks like him," Howie declared.

"Undoubtedly," was my reply. This was Woodstock and Jeanette was Jeanette. A Truman Capote look-alike, complete with shoulder bag, approached the pick-up.

"Looking in the driver's window he said, "You must be Howie and you, of course, are Jake. How lovely to meet you."

"Nice meeting you," we replied in unison.

"Welcome to Woodstock," he said. "Jake, it's fate, you know."

"How's that?" I asked.

"I have driven by your shop so many times and was just drawn to go in but never did and now here you are. You do have that distressed furniture place in New Paltz?"

"Antiques," I corrected.

"Oh yes, antiques. Well, why don't you recover your charges and you can follow me to my place?" he said, with a lecherous wink.

I was beginning to feel like an hors d'oeuvre.

CHAPTER EIGHT

March 12, 1914
The Winter Palace
St. Petersburg

The monk, as he was called, paused before beginning the descent down the great staircase of the Winter Palace. Gone was the unwashed, wandering holy man with his rough linen shirt and peasant garb. Here now was the great and powerful Rasputin; his pale yellow silk blouse was hand-embroidered by the Empress herself; black velvet trousers were tucked into his soft kid boots. A sky-blue silken cord belted his waist, from it hung long tassels; a heavy gold chain and cross around his neck completed the "habit."

But the monk's splendid appearance was over-shadowed by the sheer power of his countenance. His eyes danced as if on fire; he was wild with exuberance. Once again, he had provided his invaluable service to both Nicholas and Alexandra. Once again, he brought back from death young Alexis. Alexis the angel, the pretty boy, the heir to the Russian throne.

The Cossack sentries stared contemptuously at the frenzied cleric. But they stared in silence.

Glaring up from the bottom of the staircase stood a tall aristocrat in the blue-green uniform of the Preobrazhinsky Guard.

"Father, I see you have been to the Palace again," said the aristocrat.

"God has worked through me again to save the Russias."

"You presume much, old man."

"Watch your tongue. Do you know to whom you speak?" Rasputin descended the steps as he spoke.

"I speak to a wandering Starets who has wandered into where he does not belong. And do you know to whom you speak?"

"Yes, to an officer in the Empress' bodyguard."

"No."

"Then you are Zemstvo Trepov, boyhood friend of the Tsar."

"No."

"Then who are you, my important one?" Rasputin stopped a step or two from the bottom; the two men were face to face.

"I am the dog that sleeps by the door, sworn to protect the Romanovs, sworn to protect the Russias." A long silence followed. A Cossack off to one side, placed his hand on the hilt of his curved sword, then dropped it back.

Surely this mad monk needed to die but as a Cossack he obeyed the will of the Tsar and surely the Tsar loved this man.

The silence was broken by Rasputin's affected laugh. "Until another day," he said as he walked around the officer, his laughter echoing down the long corridors.

The officer of the Preobrazhinsky Guard Regiment stood rigidly staring ahead at the now-empty great staircase, his face crimson, the veins of his neck bulging.

CHAPTER NINE

October 5
Sumpter House
Woodstock, New York

I hadn't gotten a good look at the place when we had come in. At first glance in the dark, and the top of the mountain was dark, it looked like some small 1950's suburban row house. But was I wrong! So what else is new?

The brochure on my dresser top told the story of the Sumpter Family, the mustard people. After 1910 or so, it would be hard to find a family that didn't have a jar of Sumpter Mustard some-place in their kitchen. Well, a lot of that mustard money went into this place - their vacation house away from the heat of New York City.

Now it was a bed and breakfast run by a Truman Capote look-alike. Actually, to call this place a B & B was like calling a Rolls Royce a station car.

I walked through a series of elegant rooms and entered the tremendous, plate glass-enclosed veranda which extended from the house and hung suspended above the deep, narrow valley divided by the silver ribbon of the river far below. The view rivaled any that Switzerland had to offer. Rachel was sitting alone, transfixed by the splendor.

I waited a moment before saying, "Hi, Rachel." She turned, looking very childlike decked out in all new clothes. An over-looked price tag hung from the back of her sweater.

"Hello, Dad," she answered with some disdain. I wasn't sure if that disdain was based on my disturbing her reverie or on something more profound.

"Dad, we need to talk." My question was answered.

"Sure. You know we can always talk."

"Right," she shot back sarcastically. "What is going on here? Something's definitely going on."

"What makes you think anything is going on?" I tried to say in a light, joking manner.

"Be serious, Dad."

"Okay, Rachel, an old case from before I retired kind of got re-opened again and, well, I just have to follow through on it.

"Why drag me along?"

"Well, you're getting older now. I'd like to think of you as part of my team." I was really grasping at straws.

"Some team." After a pause she continued. "Françoise's a whore, a prostitute, isn't she?" Without waiting for a reply she went on repeating, now somewhat hysterically, "Some team, some team! A prostitute, a crazy private eye on Prozac, a retired drunk, the flaming faggot that runs this place..."

I was about to interject, "Yes, and a spoiled brat teenager," when Howie wandered in and calmly added, "She hasn't met the lady priest yet."

"Minister," I corrected. Rachel ran from the room. I felt like shit.

"Don't worry too much. She's just having her days, no doubt."

"Look, Howie..."

"Boys, boys," came the voice of Bruce Ogilvie, the real name of "Truman Capote," as he walked onto the veranda with

Jeanette, who was complete with clerical collar. "Don't be cross with each other. Here, now, you three have much to talk about. Dear Rachel seems vexed so I'll seek her assistance in preparing lunch which will be served shortly on the veranda."

With that he left the room, calling as he went down the hallway in his high-pitched voice, "Rachel, dear Rachel."

I noticed Howie taking his morning dose of medication.

Without speaking, perhaps being afraid to speak, we sat down at a small table away from the door. Jeanette spoke first, "It's going slow. I have to decrypt, decode and sometimes translate. They use a lot of one time ciphers which makes things difficult. Some stuff is in English, some in Russian and, guess what, some in Latin. But as far as I can make out at this point is that these are minutes of meetings of some council or committee of twelve. They're moving large amounts of money offshore to the U.S. and some from the U.S. to Russia. Some big event is coming up, I think in Europe, probably Russia, and they're getting ready to make some kind of move. The term "Pretty Boy" keeps cropping up, which I presume to be a code name of someone, but maybe not. Bruce has some experience and a home computer and we are going to work on this today and have whatever answers we can give you by tonight. Bruce is going to have a couple of his, eh, friends over to help keep an eye on things."

"Is that necessary?" Howie asked.

"All very low-key. I trust there are funds available to cover necessary expenses?"

"Within reason," Howie said, showing more business acumen than I had given him credit for.

"Jake, I am also concerned about Rachel. She's at such a delicate age and, well, maybe..."

"I'll admit that things with her and me are a little shaky."

Jeanette continued, "It's time that you filled me in on what you are working on."

"An Admiral Sam Jeffries," Howie began, "was about to retire and got approached by some historical foundation which was apparently a front for some kind of intelligence operation. The money was good but it smelled bad so, for whatever reason, he was doing his own free-lance counter-operation. But he buys the farm, au natural, while in the sack with a pro who's upstairs now. All hell breaks loose, bodies start popping up. We're doing damage control re: the Admiral's good name and trying to find out who the bad guys are and what they're up to."

"Got you."

I was again surprised at how succinctly Howie summed up the relevant facts. I saw Rachel come back into the room. In the doorway stood Bruce.

"She's gone."

CHAPTER TEN

June 3, 1914
St. Petersburg

He, Grigory Rasputin, came out of the obscurity of Siberia with no more than rags on his back. Now he was the great monk who wore silk and gold and advised the Tsar of all the Russias on all matters, spiritual and political. Now he was one of the most powerful men in Russia and therefore, perhaps he thought, indirectly one of the most powerful in the world.

He could live in the great Winter Palace or in any of the Tsar's other palaces, for that matter, if he chose to. He could live where he wanted and he wanted to live beyond the Kazan Gates on Meshchanskaya Street. There were some fine houses and apartments on Meshchanskaya Street but Rasputin chose to live among the tobacconists and grocery shops in a run-down rooming house on the poorest section of the street. Not that he came to his room there every night, but tonight he was on his way there, walking alone down Meshchanskaya Street. Walking alone as always, refusing the company of the Court appointed attendant or Cossack body guard.

Rasputin was drunk but continued to stop at each vodka seller on the street. Foreigners were always amazed at how many establishments sold strong drink on the streets of St. Petersburg and Moscow.

To the foreign diplomats and visiting European aristocrats at the Russian Court, Rasputin was an enigma. They all recognized that this mad monk was either a dangerous adversary or, if compromised in some fashion, a useful pawn. The visiting dignitaries were drawn by fascination with him. The mystique of Rasputin was not unlike that of Merlin at the Court of King Arthur. He was the finishing touch in making the Romanov Court a throw-back to medieval times, times when aristocrats held their secure place of privilege and well-being. It was no wonder that the Russians looked back in time, for this new century, this Twentieth Century seemed to no longer even tolerate them.

Whether perceived as an angel or devil, the Russian aristocrat and peasant alike understood Rasputin. As God came to man in the form of Christ, so did Rasputin embody the soul of the Russian peasant and it was the peasant that was the very essence of Russia.

Staggering, Rasputin banged the door open and entered the dim, candle-lit kitchen of the rooming house. It smelled of cabbage, onions, and stale alcohol. His wife Praskovie sat at the battered table sipping hot, sweet tea from a glass.

"Close the door, Grigory, the night air is damp," she said, "and be quiet about it. The others are asleep."

"What do I care for the others? I am Rasputin, advisor and confidant of the Tsar."

"That may be at the Palace but here you are my husband, Grigory, my husband who is a drunk."

"Be still, woman," Rasputin said as he closed the door with the slow deliberation that a drunk needs to accomplish simple tasks. He dropped himself into a chair opposite his wife and continued, "Why do you sit up and drink tea, waiting for me? Is it that you desire me like the women at the Court?"

"No, my dear husband, Grigory. Your charms have never

been lost on me but not worth waiting up for."

"Then what do you want of me tonight? I am tired and need to sleep."

"I have a message for you. The Prince was here tonight."

"What prince?"

"My dear husband deals with so many princes, he needs to ask which one?"

"You anger me. Speak plainly."

"Feliks Yusupov, the great prince. He wanted your advice. He thought perhaps you would ride with him in his carriage, better to have your undivided attention."

"Better that he and his friends can do away with me."

"My husband, the dull-witted prophet, you advise the Tsar but don't accept the danger around you. You underestimate your enemies and that is the mark of a fool, not a prophet."

"Underestimate them? No, no, my dear. It is they who underestimate me. I tell you now it is Yusupov who will succeed where others have failed. It is by his hand I will die."

"If that be true, then prevent it."

"No need, my dearest, when this body is gone I have devised a way for my work to carry on. Just as the Tsar or any government has a council of ministers, now so have I. My council, twelve of them whom I have appointed, twelve - did you hear that? - will rule in my absence."

"A lot of good that will do you."

Seeking simply to best him on some point, she said, "Yes, but whatever your plans, if Russia is crushed in the war, what then?"

"Woman, even in my presence, you cannot see the greatness. I have made powerful allies in other countries, especially, especially, in the Tsarina's native Germany. Beyond that, throughout the entire world, there are others who think the same. You know me better than anyone yet you understand me the least. You should realize I will be back, again and again. So let them kill me." He buried his head in his arms on the table and fell into a deep sleep.

She mused to herself that he was right again, he was always right. The better she knew him, the less she understood him. She remembered him as a young man in Siberia, a charlatan. She was his accomplice in his petty swindles. When he began to play the rôle of a sage, his prophecies came true, but only because he was lucky or they together had manipulated the outcome. It had been the same with his healings.

But now it was as if he could actually foresee the future - no - control the future was more like it. Had he become a prophet; was he always one and they just had not known it or was she finally succumbing to his mesmerizing?

'I can't explain it,' Praskovie thought wearily as she climbed the stairs to bed, 'but he is always right.'

****

Prince Yusupov sat in the smoking room outside of the wine cellar under his family home in St. Petersburg. Grand Duke Dmitry Pavlovich, the Emperor's nephew, Vladimir Mitrofanovich Purishkevich, a Duma member, and Dr. Lazovert sat with him, all downing flutes of peppered vodka.

Purishkevich was the drunkest. "I never could understand. That's why I never took him seriously. An uneducated peasant from Siberia, not even a legitimate Starets. A peasant who becomes a holy man. This Rasputin is nothing more than a lunatic, charlatan member of the Khlysty cult. Lunatics, all of them, flagellating each other and God only knows what else. And now he controls the Russian Court and our destiny."

"Shut up," Lazovert said. Lazovert was probably only a little less intoxicated. "We know with what we are dealing. We are here to decide how and when to end this obscenity."

"I agree," Pavlovich said, "but what of the Tsarina? Her

dependence upon this mad monk in all things is beyond reason. To kill him will bring death to all of us, not that I any longer care, but it will be the last straw in the stability of the Tsar's reign when there are both so many internal and external pressures, not just on the Tsar but the very Monarchy."

"Pavlovich, have faith in your uncle. He can control his wife and truly the two love each other, regardless of this mad man. It is the child that raises the question, the problem."

"Yes, Alexis, the heir, the bleeder. How is it that this mad monk controls the disease of the boy? If we save the Tsar and lose the boy, all is lost anyway. Is there nothing that we can offer this mad monk simply to have him quietly disappear? He has made his fortune, slept with half the women at the court. He can have whatever he wants..."

"Purishkevich, don't be a fool. Are we too being seduced by the trickery of this rogue? He has no power to save the life of the child and that will be clear when he is gone. What he wants is what we have always had and are losing to him - power."

"Yes, power but respect, too," whispered Pavlovich.

"What difference does it make?" said Prince Yusupov. "Without action, all is lost. We have no choice but to act. Sometime, we will gather with him in this room and he will meet his destiny with the poison I shall give him, just as he has poisoned the mind of our beloved Empress."

CHAPTER ELEVEN

October 5
Sumpter House
Woodstock

Rachel was right. Françoise was gone. Besides concern, I also felt a sense of betrayal. I had lost objectivity, lines and rôles had blurred. I realized that I had been operating like the mother hen to some dysfunctional family. It was time to start acting like an intelligence officer again. Yeah, my daughter was visiting but that relationship had to be put on hold until the operation was over. It was too bad that most of her life circumstances like this had always made me put our relationship on hold, but it was too late to look back.

I'm not sure why, maybe it was for parity with Howie, maybe it was because I missed it, maybe it was because things were getting hairy; I don't know, but it was time to start carrying again. There was no doubt in my mind that Bruce, our host, could and would accommodate me. Nonetheless, I was a bit taken aback when he showed me into a walk-in-closet-turned-armory. An amazing assortment of weapons were neatly lined up in racks or on shelves.

Bruce said, "Shall I recommend something or do you have a preference?"

It was like he was selling washing machines. "Do you have a government .45 auto?" I asked.

"Certainly. A good choice. I can see you are a traditionalist."

Not only did I come out with the .45 but a Bianchi belt holster, a box of 50 cartridges, and an extra magazine. It was sort of like getting a K-Mart "Blue Light Special."

Without any apologies, I told Jeanette to look after Rachel, and Howie and I struck out to find the wayward Françoise.

A flash of Howie's badge matched with a display of my old Naval ID, which somehow I had neglected to turn in, gave us the trail - a taxi from Woodstock to Kingston and a Trailways bus to New York City. Françoise had rabbited. She was headed for home - a BIG mistake.

All things considered, we couldn't be that far behind her. Howie did 85 most of the way down the New York State Thruway. I expected the truck's engine to fly out at any minute.

Howie and I had usually driven around in silence, but this time there was a lot of conversation. He told a lot of war stories about his days in the ONI and N.S.A. Stories that probably were designed to provide me with insights into his rather complex personality.

"My excuse for smoking weed," he said, "is it keeps me from drinking booze. I had about a dozen reasons for drinking when I did but mostly it was lifestyle. It kind of came with the territory. What's your reason?" he asked in a non-judgmental way.

"I used to say it saved my life."

"How's that?"

"Well, during my first tour in Nam, I was in Zumwalt's Riverine Force; I was one of those Ensign Captains of a fiberglass patrol boat on the Mekong. Pretty bizarre duty."

"And nasty," Howie commented as if thinking aloud.

"Well, I was still drinking like a college fraternity brother and one night I passed out in the New York Club in Saigon."

"That was the place run by the old Special Forces guy on TuDo Street."

"Yeah, that's the place."

"It had that huge mahogany bar."

"Yeah, mahogany and teak. That's what saved me. I was passed out lying on the floor behind the bar the night the V.C. blew the place. A combination of being flat on the floor and that massive bar, well, I made it when a lot of less drunk guys didn't."

"Interesting."

"Yeah, but the truth is, it is the lifestyle to a large degree."

****

We got to the apartment building and cruised the neighborhood. Nothing leaped out at us, so we went into the building. Neither the doorman nor the concierge were in the lobby. It saved the tiresome flash of ID but raised the spectre that something was amiss.

We went upstairs and stopped in front of her door. Howie glanced at me before knocking. He knocked lightly. He attempted but failed to achieve an equal lightness in his voice when he called out, "Hi there. Anyone home?" As he spoke, he twisted the knob of the unlocked door.

Immediately from the inside came the familiar voice of Françoise. "It's open, come in."

Another glance from Howie. With his left hand he slowly opened the door; positioning himself sideways, his right hand withdrew a Smith and Wesson model 59 automatic from beneath his corduroy jacket. I stepped back behind the door frame, my right hand instinctively went to the butt of my holstered .45. I felt the powerful mixed sensations of fear and excitement as adrenaline pumped into my system. The door swung fully open.

Françoise was sitting rigidly in a red velvet, high backed chair. She smelled of terror but was calm. It looked as if she'd been sitting there for a while. We came through the door. Howie kicked it shut with the back of his foot.

"Hi, Françoise," I said.

She answered only with her eyes, glancing towards the kitchen area. No one was in sight but you could feel his presence. We moved a few steps forward to meet him, or maybe them.

In a flash, they were on us. Black streaks, all teeth and fur. Like banshees, the two animals literally flew from the bedroom. Howie went down. The German Shepherd on him had lunged for his gun hand before knocking him to the ground. His pistol skidded across the tile floor. In that split second, I was down, too. It was a savage wrestling match with quick silver. I had both hands on the beast's neck. Its front paws clawed at my face. Escape became my only thought.

I was vaguely aware of the sharp crack that, as if by some black art, made the head of the dog disintegrate. The headless animal dropped off me like so much dead weight. Covered with blood and gore, I staggered to my feet. Howie was already up; at his feet lay the other now headless German Shepherd. His left arm hung limp and bloody, his familiar brown corduroy jacket in shreds. He picked up a heavy table lamp, yanking the cord from the outlet. Holding it upside down, he advanced slowly and menacingly towards the man who had emerged from the kitchen, nervously holding a 9 mm Beretta. I moved to the right and pulled my .45. I felt my left hand touching the blood on my face. Howie noticed Françoise out of the corner of his eye. She was resolutely holding his gun, the magic instrument that could disintegrate the heads of dogs. Holding it at arm's length, she pointed it towards the man with the Beretta.

Howie angrily threw the lamp to the floor and moved to the left. Gently he reached out and took his gun back from her extended hand. Howie moved towards the adversary, stepping over a coffee table. He paused by the stereo system. Following

Howie's lead, Françoise picked up the discarded lamp and held it threateningly. The eyes of the man with the Beretta darted back and forth between Howie, Françoise, and myself. He threw the Beretta down and raised his hands. Evidently, he was alone.

Howie studied the stereo for a moment then touched a few buttons. Françoise fell back into the velvet chair, still holding the lamp. The voice of National Public Radio filled the room with the announcement that the next number would be the original Glenn Miller Orchestra playing, "Puttin' on the Ritz." Howie nodded in approval and started advancing on the obviously frightened stranger.

Almost comically, the radio blared out, "Do do do, do do dat do, do do do do, do do dat do..., puttin' on the Ritz." Howie, limp arm bleeding, smiled as he advanced. The man shrank in terror. Slowly bending down, Howie picked up the Beretta from the floor with his left hand and, with some difficulty, he stuck it in his belt. As he stood up - BLAM - he almost casually shot the man in the left knee. The man slammed against the wall and collapsed, screaming; his leg grotesquely pointed in the wrong direction, like a bent rag doll. "Do do do do, do do dat do, puttin' on the Ritz."

Françoise began to laugh hysterically. I suspected it was a result of frenzy rather than an appreciation of the black humor.

"Mother-fucker, you shot me. Son of a bitch, I'm dying. Mother-fucker."

"Not dying, just crippled."

"Christ, get me to a doctor. Mother-fucker."

"Do do dat do, puttin' on the Ritz."

I stood transfixed; Françoise laughed on.

"Okay pal, here goes the other one," Howie declared, aiming at the other knee.

"Jesus, don't shoot, please man, please, get me a doctor."

Howie looked at his gun as if to see if it was still working, then announced, "Handicap accessible, here you come!"

"Don't shoot, man! What do you want? Just tell me what you want.'

"That's the spirit. Jake, fix up his leg will ya?"

I went into the bathroom and found some sanitary napkins. I pulled off the wrappers and pushed a bunch of them against the bleeding mess that had been a knee. Howie was pouring gin down the wounded man's throat. He stood up and pulled the table cloth off the kitchen table; artificial flowers, salt and pepper shakers, and other miscellaneous items went flying. I wrapped the bloody leg with the cloth.

"Do do do, do do dat do, puttin' on the Ritz."

"Well folks, that was Glenn Miller and "Puttin' on the Ritz."

Howie stood up and shot the stereo. He was one sick puppy. Françoise stopped laughing.

"Who do you work for?" Howie asked.

"The Major."

"The Major? Major who?" I asked.

"He is a Major in the A.O.B."

"A.O.B.?" I said. "What the hell is that?"

"Aryan Order Brotherhood, a paramilitary, white supremacist group," Howie answered off-handedly.

"I don't know his name, man. He's some kind of Neo-Nazi freak, with a lot of money. Are you gonna get me to the hospital, man?"

"Sure," said Howie, picking up the telephone. With his thumb holding down the disconnect button, he spoke into the receiver, "911? Get an ambulance up to 1150 Park Avenue, apartment 812. Yeah, a gunshot wound." He hung up the phone. Walking over to Françoise, he knelt down next to her and gently took the lamp. "How're you doing, honey?"

"Okay," she said.

"Look," I pressed on with the wounded man, "how long you been working for the Major?"

"About two months."

"Where do you know him from?"

"I got hooked up with him through the magazine."

I would have pursued that one but knew we were running out of time. "What's this all about?" I took a shot at one last question.

"Man, is the ambulance coming?"

"Answer his question," Howie snarled.

"I don't know. It's a CIA thing. You know, to take over the government in Russia. Man, get the ambulance to hurry."

The ambulance wasn't coming but by now half the New York City Police Department was. While Howie talked to Françoise, I went through the wounded man's jacket pockets. I took out a car rental contract, his wallet, keys to the rental car and a parking garage receipt. In his shirt pocket was a now useless dog whistle.

"Françoise," Howie said, "where the hell did you learn to shoot like that?"

"Howie," she said, "I've got to tell you something, sort of a confession." I heard what she said and braced myself for some awesome revelation.

"Howie," she said again, "Howie, I'm not really French."

"You're not?" he said, feigning great surprise.

"No, I'm not, and Françoise is not my real name."

"It's not?" Howie said, maintaining the surprise in his voice.

"Neither is LaTrec." Evidently Françoise, or whatever her name was, was breaking the news to us in easy stages.

"What is your name?" Howie asked.

" Tammy, Tammy Jane Martin."

"Well, Tammy Jane is a nice name but where did you learn to shoot like that?"

"I grew up on a farm in Kansas. Can you imagine that - not Paris, Kansas. My brothers and me used to shoot coyotes, and coons, and deer, and rabbits, and squirrels and possums and..."

Thinking the litany was unending, I cut in, "Look you two,

let's get out of here."

"Get out of here?" said the wounded man. "Where's my ambulance?"

"It's coming," the three of us said in unison.

"Come on, Howie, let's go."

"Take it easy, Jake. Look, Françoise, we're still going to call you that, okay?"

'That was good,' I thought. This whole thing was bizarre enough without people starting to change their names, but it seemed Howie's motivation was more esoteric.

"Look, Françoise, what do you know about reincarnation?"

"Ah, come on, Howie, let's get out of here."

"Shut up, Jake." He was really angry at me now. It was best to let him do his thing and hope for the best. I was dealing with a real lunatic.

"Isn't that when you die you become someone else?" Françoise asked.

"Sort of," Howie answered.

With the greatest tenderness, Howie explained, "You're the same person, the same soul, and your soul is French. This time you just happened to be born in Kansas - but you are 100% French."

"You think so?" she asked hopefully.

"I know so," Howie said with the conviction of the Pope.

"But Howie, there's something else. There's something else about me you have to know. It's really terrible although sometimes I think it might be good. There's something else you should know about me."

"Howie," I said quietly.

"Okay," he said, "let's go. We'll talk later, honey." He helped Françoise up and, turning to the wounded man, aimed his Smith and Wesson at the center of his chest.

"Oh God," said the crippled man as he attempted to crawl backwards.

I really think Howie would have shot him if Françoise hadn't gently but firmly pulled his arm down. There were sounds of activity in the hall outside.

I reached into Howie's torn jacket and pulled out his New York Detective shield which I clipped onto Françoise's collar. I clipped my Navy ID to my jacket and, putting Howie's arms around our shoulders, opened the door. Uniformed City cops with drawn revolvers were entering the hall from the stairs and elevators.

"We've got an officer down here. Get out of the way." I holstered my .45 and stuck Howie's piece in my belt. "Call down and check on the paramedics. Hold that elevator. I've got a perp down in there. The others headed for the roof."

With that, two uniformed cops reached for Howie; the real blood on his arm was convincing, his muttering, "Mother, Mother," was not, but the cops were caught up in the moment. Half the uniforms headed for the roof, the others entered the apartment. To one still in the hallway, I handed the Beretta that I had removed from Howie's belt and, with an official casualness, said, "Do me a favor and voucher this."

From inside the apartment, I heard the wounded man yell, "Is my ambulance here?"

"Shut up, scumbag," came the reply of the uniformed officer, believing he was talking to a cop shooter.

It took some doing and a couple of times I didn't think we were going to make it but we managed to slip away and headed for the garage where the wounded man's car, hopefully, was.

Howie waited down the street while Françoise and I got the car, a nondescript Chrysler product.

After picking up some peroxide for Howie's arm, we headed back to Woodstock. Françoise, A.K.A. Tammy Jane, promised not to run away again. Maybe we were making progress.

PART III

THE MONK

"When someone is honestly 55% right, that's very good and there's no use wrangling. And if someone is 60% right, it's wonderful, it's great luck, and let him thank God. But what's to be said about 75% right? Wise people say this is suspicious. Well and what about 100% right? Whoever says he's 100% right is a fanatic, a thug, and the worst kind of rascal."

An Old Jew of Galatia

CHAPTER TWELVE

July 27, 1914
The Winter Palace
St. Petersburg

The mauve boudoir of the Empress Alexandra was her private preserve. Rarely did the Emperor visit that sanctuary, and never without advance notice, but the door was always open to her spiritual advisor, her confessor, "Father" Rasputin - the Mad Monk, as many in the Duma were beginning to call him.

The Empress lay back on her fainting couch as the monk in his resplendent attire paced the floor. Even Alexandra had begun to fear this man's intensity. She mentally searched for a way to end his tirade. Suddenly, Rasputin stopped and stared towards the heavens as if hearing a message no one else could. The Empress seized the moment.

"Dearest Father, I will take your concerns to Papa."

"I have written Papa," Rasputin spat back. "To what end? Your husband has turned against me, his mind poisoned by my enemies, just as I told you it would happen, did I not?"

"Yes, Father, but..."

"But what? What have I prophesied that has not come to pass?" Not waiting for an answer he continued, "And why is this?"

Perhaps out of belief, perhaps because it was the expected answer, the Empress intoned, "Because God speaks through you."

"Yes, but not for the benefit of me, but for the benefit of Russia. Is that not so?"

"Yes, Father."

"I tell you war is coming and with it will come the end of this divine monarchy. Chaos will reign. That is why the boy must be saved."

"But Father, the Kaiser and Papa are cousins. Doubtlessly reason will prevail; and cannot Russia defend itself with its armies?"

Rasputin stared down at the Empress until she cast her eyes to the floor. As he began to speak again he drew a scroll of papers from his flowing sleeve. "Listen, woman, as the Bible was written with divine inspiration, so I have written this. It is the plan that has been put in place to save the pretty boy. As Joseph was sent into exile to be in a position to save the people of Israel many years later so will Alexis someday return to save the Rodina, our great motherland Russia, and the House of Romanov. So God wills."

In a violent gesture, the monk threw the scroll onto the couch, hitting the Empress in the leg. Abruptly, as if suddenly seeming satisfied with himself, Rasputin turned and left the boudoir.

A fierce temper raged in the mind of the Empress Alexandra. Regardless of whom or what this man was or what she felt towards him, no one spoke to the Empress in that manner, let alone strike her, however lightly.

For the first time she understood why so many wanted this man destroyed but maybe, just maybe, he was right. She placed the scroll on the bottom of her jewelry box.

****

Finally, the night came and Pavlovich, Purishkevich, Lazovert, Prince Yusupov and Rasputin did meet and, to the shock of all present, the poison in the cakes and wine did not kill but only served to anger the monk who had become the de facto ruler of Russia.

Enraged, Rasputin overturned the furniture and attacked Yusupov. Pavlovich emptied his revolver at close range into the mad monk's chest, to no effect.

Prince Yusupov drew his dagger and stabbed deep into what he thought was his attacker's heart. Purishkevich bludgeoned the monk over the head with a fireplace iron. Rasputin sank to the floor but he seemed to be passing out more from the vodka he had consumed than from the deadly blows he had received.

Wrapping his body in a carpet, the conspirators took the still breathing Rasputin to the nearly frozen Neva River and tossed him into the freezing water. Although weighted down, the body rose to the surface, through the ice, and Rasputin appeared to be swimming before disappearing into the downstream darkness.

Soon there would be sitings of Rasputin throughout St. Petersburg and Moscow and the legend of his immortality would be born.

CHAPTER THIRTEEN

October 6
Cambridge, Saratoga County
New York

Crossing the Hudson at Schuylerville, he drove south on Route 24 to Greenwich, admiring as always the magnificent Victorian homes of that town. Turning onto 372, he continued the familiar trip through the countryside which has been called a nineteenth century *Peaceable Kingdom*.

Coming into Cambridge, he turned right, noticing the sign that pointed the way to Grandma Moses' Home a few miles further south at the next exit down the road in the Town of Hoosic Falls. In a few minutes, he pulled into the parking lot below the sign that read, *The Monks of New Skete*.

The man got out of the car and walked up the brick path through the grove of oak trees. Rounding the corner, a small, beautiful Russian Orthodox Church came into view. The traditional timber sides reached up to the steeply slanted roof topped with golden onion domes. The building's simple beauty inevitably created a sense of reverence in even the most callous tourist.

The man paused to look at the church and then turned down

the path to the kennels of the Monastery's dog obedience school. He stopped to inspect the display case of photographs of famous people with their dogs which had been trained there. Prominently displayed were photos of Alexander Solzhenitsyn's animal which had been trained by the monks in the Russian tongue.

In a few moments, he was approached by a short, stocky man of about 60 years, unremarkable in appearance save for the neatly trimmed mustache and goatee.

"Good morning, Carl," said the goateed man.

"Good morning, Doctor. It's a grand day, is it not?"

"I suspect that your exuberance transcends the weather."

"And why shouldn't it? Have you good news for me?"

"Yes, Carl. As they say, trite but true, *A picture is worth a thousand words*, and a video, well..." With that, the bearded doctor handed a nylon airline shoulder bag to the other man.

Carl slung the bag over his shoulder and asked, "The videos are good and usable?"

"We couldn't ask for anything better. They are pure artistry, they are my masterpieces. The appeal will be to Nationalists, Monarchists, Socialists, the potentially religious, to every faction, to every person - perfect."

"But is the boy credible?" interrupted Carl. "And what about public appearances?"

"It is his credibility that makes the videos work and I am convinced that we can handle a live appearance."

"Pavlov is rolling in his grave," interjected Carl. "You have done well, more than well, and it is appreciated. Name your reward. Remember that I am one of the senior-most Council members. You have only to ask."

"Simply remember our bargain, our agreement."

"You will have that and more, Doctor." With that he turned and began to retrace his steps back up the path.

"Carl," called the doctor, "our enemies are getting close."

"Not to worry. They will be too late," Carl called over his shoulder as he disappeared from view into the oak grove.

CHAPTER FOURTEEN

March 12, 1917
Tsarskoe Selo
Russia

Some fifteen miles south of St. Petersburg lay the iron-fence-enclosed thousand acre park known as the Tsar's Village. A fairy tale paradise that generations of Tsars had built as a sort of private World's Fair, complete with Chinese pagodas, Turkish baths, Alpine lakes and exotic flowers; the entire compound was constantly patrolled by colorful but deadly Cossacks. It was here that the Empress had taken refuge. The Tsar, the Autocrat of all the Russias, had abdicated and was a prisoner of the Revolution at what had been the Imperial Headquarters on the German Front.

In the drawing room turned hospital of the Palace, Lili Dehn, the Empress' oldest and closest friend, nursed four of the five royal children, Olga, Tatiana, Anastasia, and the Crown Prince, Alexis. They had been suffering from fevers brought on by measles.

It was late in the afternoon when the Empress returned in her Red Cross uniform from her meeting with the officers of the Palace Guard.

"Lil," she said, "it is very bad. The Litovsky Regiment has mutinied and murdered their officers; the Volinsky Regiment followed suit. I can't understand it. I was always afraid but never really, really believed in the possibility of Revolution but it has come."

"He was right, you know," answered Lili.

"He was always right, but he is gone."

"Which, too, he foresaw. What is there to do? If only his power could reach beyond the grave."

"Perhaps it has," noted the Empress. "Lili, find Derevenko and bring him to me in the Chapel quickly. There may not be much time."

Derevenko came and bowed to the Empress. As always he wore the simple sailor's uniform of the Imperial Navy. Derevenko had been taken years ago from the ranks to be the protector of the Crown Prince. Not the body guard, that was a function of the Cossacks, but the protector to save the always sickly Alexis from childhood injuries that might be fatal to the hemophiliac heir to the throne.

"Seaman Derevenko, you must again protect the heir. You must take him away to safety."

"But Your Majesty, surely the child is safe here in the Tsar's own village with 1,500 loyal men of the Garde Equipage surrounding us. Imperial troops still hold the Winter Palace and soon the Tsar himself will return. Then all will be well."

"The Tsar is no more. He is now simply Nicholas Romanov."

"Your Highness, I will give my life for the child but I am not a warrior, select an officer from the Cossack Regiment."

"No, Derevenko, no one loves the child as you, no one."

Derevenko cast his eyes to the floor and pondered the Empress' statement. "I am your servant, Your Highness."

"Take this package. Do not deviate in any way from its instructions. I shall go now and say good-bye to my son."

"I shall give my life, Your Highness."

As the Empress Alexandra of Russia left the simple seaman in the Palace Chapel she thought sadly to herself, 'And so you shall. And now, I must choose a child from one of the peasant families in the compound to serve as a sacrifice for my son.'

****

It had been a long and dangerous trip. The journey had covered more than miles, it seemed to traverse time itself. It began in the sophistication and luxury of Tsarskoe Selo and ended on the bleak, harsh, primeval steppes of Siberia. It had begun in a place where the Romanov Dynasty was becoming history but finished where Nicholas was still the Tsar and Emperor. At first, the Imperial Seaman Derevenko and the Russian heir traveled incognito, at night, by horse-drawn cart. But, the further from Moscow the two traveled, the more open they could and did become. Derevenko used the official papers, orders and money provided him to finally allow the boy to travel in the way and manner befitting his status. Never once did Derevenko let down his guard.

It was only in the last few miles that Derevenko again began to grow apprehensive. Surely it had been that mad monk, Rasputin, who had chosen the Monastery of Verkhoturye as the refuge of the heir, Alexis.

Certainly, this place could not be his final destination. He was certain he would receive new orders and resources here to take the child on to a final destination - perhaps the Crimea or even England.

A well-known retreat for ordained monks, Verkhoturye had a darker side as well. It was a place of confinement for members of heretical sects, particularly for followers of the Khlysty Way. The Khlysty cult believed in a very pagan way in spiritual growth through sexual ritual and abandonment. It had always been rumored that Rasputin had begun his career as a Khlysty, a story Derevenko now was sure was true. It was a safe place to stop but he was glad when the Abbot confirmed that the boy would soon be moving on.

"Go Derevenko, and sleep deeply, you have done well. All will be safe here for a while but soon the pretty one will move on to yet a safer," he paused, then continued, "and more appropriate haven."

Derevenko bowed and went to his sleeping chamber. He was both proud and relieved at having brought the child through to safety. He lay back and drifted into a deep sleep, a sleep from which he never awoke. Derevenko, the simple seaman who loved the boy, never felt the wire garrote that took his life.

****

It took well more than two years for the Crown Prince Alexis Romanov to be taken in stages to a safe and secluded place well out of the reach of the growing revolution. Each time he arrived at a new way-station, his guides made the same sacrifice as Derevenko. Sometimes staying days, weeks, or even months at a monastery, diplomatic residence, or the home of some loyal or corruptible official, the boy progressed slowly but inexorably to the planned safe haven. There could be no trail. He or his progeny would be safe until the time was right to return.

CHAPTER FIFTEEN

October 5
Sumpter House
Woodstock

I was glad to get back to Woodstock and the Sumpter House. The place was not only magnificent and peaceful but was also safe. It was like a Castle with the draw-bridge up. In our absence, the castle had been manned by a strange assortment of knights. Manned was probably a poor choice of words.

A dozen or so obviously gay men had taken up residence as a sort of informal security force. A few body-builders lifted weights in the driveway near where a couple of martial arts types exercised. Particularly fascinating was a leotard-clad fellow practicing with a cross-bow. I was told a couple of armed cohorts patrolled the woods. Still others lounged around the house reading a variety of literature.

While all were clearly gay, none were particularly effeminate except for the one who seemed to be the unit's medic. Effeminate or not, he skillfully treated Howie's arm.

Rachel was content, as content as I had ever seen her. She mostly stayed in the kitchen, cooking and baking under the tutelage of our host, Bruce.

Jeanette stayed on the veranda decoding, translating a word here and there, and trying to plug them into possible sentences. Françoise had a few drinks and went to bed early. She seemed relaxed, almost relieved, that her secret was out. Maybe she had bought into Howie's theory of a French soul or maybe she related to the fairy tale environment of the Sumpter House. No pun intended.

Under the watchful eye of the martial artists, Howie and I searched the rental car. Thankfully Howie was not at all upset about having had to abandon his pick-up in the City.

The only things in the car were a couple of copies of *Soldier of Fortune* magazine lying on the front seat and an Egyptian-made semi-automatic AK-47 Kalashnikov in the trunk. With the Kalashnikov were several loaded thirty-round magazines.

Howie made a couple of calls to research the information in the car rental contract. It turned out to have been rented by the Southern Cross Corporation out of Rising Sun, Maryland.

In the classified section of one of the Soldier of Fortune magazines was an ad which read:

> *Experienced mercenaries wanted*
> *Skilled personnel only*
> *For domestic and foreign operations*
> *Reply with complete resume:*
>   *The Major*
>   *P.O. Box 819*
>   *Rising Sun, MD 21911*

"So this must be the magazine our friend was talking about," Howie said almost absentmindedly.

"I wonder if he ever got his ambulance?" I asked.

"Are you kidding me? Not in New York. The poor fool's probably still lying there."

"I hope he likes the life of a mercenary."

"Arm chair adventurers. Assholes, all of them," Howie said with disdain.

"You know, Howie, there's been nothing on the news about our ah..."

"Rescue of Françoise," chuckled Howie.

"Whatever. But someone has the ability and the desire to keep a lid on things." I wondered if they were sanitizing the apartment with new carpets again and speculated that perhaps our tax dollars were at work.

"Yeah, Jake, and whoever they are, they're watching every move real close."

"Yeah. I'm getting the decided impression that our rôle is sort of a running target to draw the bad guys out."

"The question is, who are the bad guys?" Howie added philosophically. "More than drawing someone out, I think we were meant to stumble into something and maybe screw it up."

"I almost forgot." I reached into my jacket pocket and took out the thin, nylon, camouflage wallet that we had taken from the wounded man. Looking through it, I felt like a kid searching some forbidden place.

A Florida driver's license identified the owner as John W. Fredericks of Fort Lauderdale. There was also a medical information card, and some dime store machine photos of him with a rather homely-looking female. I counted eight $100 bills and a few singles. I split it with Howie.

"I see you're learning," he said, more pleased with my attitude than in actually receiving the money.

In the wallet was a telephone number jotted on a torn paper napkin. Pay dirt. Howie and I walked back towards the house.

"What do you make of our host?" asked Howie quietly.

"Beats me. When I got the .45 from him, I had the distinct impression that I was renting it. You know, Howie, I've never rented a gun before."

"Yeah, and what do you make of the high-heeled storm troopers? Reminds me of the joke when I was a kid about the two queers - that's what we called them then, remember? Well anyway, they were walking down by the river and one says, "Look at the ferry boat," and the other says, "I knew there were a lot of us but I didn't think we had our own Navy." Howie laughed at his own joke then continued, "Now they've got their own Army, too."

"Getting back to the point, Howie, I don't think this place, these guys and my .45 are coming cheap. Who's going to foot the bill?"

"Don't worry, there are a lot of deep pockets around."

CHAPTER SIXTEEN

December 20, 1941
Village of Ialos
Greece

The American contemplated the name of the village as he walked up the dirt road. Translated, Ialos meant "shore" but the town, such as it was, lay deep in the interior and towards the north, nowhere near the sea. 'Just like these crazy Greeks,' he thought, 'to name a mountain town after the seashore.'

Of the two roads leaving Ialos, this one wound its way up the mountain the locals called "One Arm." The mountain, peculiarly bald, took its name from the solitary fig tree which clung to the side of the trail near the top. The ancient tree had one arm-like, long branch pointing with sinister foreboding the way to the dilapidated church and mysterious monastery, which housed the only residents of this great hill, long steeped in mysticism.

As the hiker approached the massive cloister door, he hid the limp from his blistered feet caused by his expensive dress shoes. This was no time to show any weakness. A small sign in Cyrillic letters spelled out *Our Lady of the Many Waters*, an accommodation of Christianity and ancient Greek paganism.

The great oak door swung open and a traditionally robed monk led the visitor in silence to the Abbot's office.

'Good theatrics,' mused the man, 'they could see me coming a mile down the road.' He wondered if it was true that the monks here enforced their vow of silence by permanently severing their vocal cords. But there was no mistaking the severed right index finger. No accident, rather an amputation to prevent betrayal by the written word, an act more symbolic than practical. 'Real fanatics,' he thought with some disgust.

The Abbot was seated behind an oak desk, sorting through papers. He looked up only after the visitor had been seated and the monk had left, closing the door behind him.

Dispelling the myth of severed vocal cords, the Abbot spoke, "I trust that your journey was not too arduous."

"Immaterial. It was a necessary one," answered the visitor.

"It would appear so," replied the Abbot enigmatically.

"To the point, Father, I have come for the child, as you are already aware."

"Yes. An action of which I do not approve."

"Again, immaterial. The decision has been made and approved by the Council."

"Ah, yes, the Council. I must tell you, just the other day I had to reprimand Brother Bartholomew. He brought a communication to me from the Council and after decoding and translating, the word Council in one place had changed into Club. Obviously an error on his part but curious nonetheless, was it not?"

"Yes, thought-provoking even," said the visitor, attempting to head off potential conflict, "but just that, an error nothing more," he continued, thinking to himself, 'How appropriate - a Club just like the Athletic Club or the Yacht Club or any of the University Clubs - only we were the most exclusive and undoubtedly the wealthiest club in New York City: The Rasputin Club.'

"I see I have lost you in thought," interrupted the Abbot. Continuing almost absentmindedly he added, "But the boy is not well."

Suddenly becoming gentler in both voice and demeanor, the visitor said, "Father, the times are insecure. The truth is, there is more danger now than ever before, even than in the old days. Now with war between Germany and the United States, well..."

"I understand but how is it you travel here in a country that has been occupied by both Italy and Germany? The troops are constantly on the roads."

"That is why our beloved founder provided us with great resources. I travel under a Swiss passport. We also have well-placed friends in the Ahnewerbe SS who are answerable only to Heinrich Himmler, Hitler's closest advisor."

'The Ahnewerbe SS' the visitor mused, 'are mere amateurs at the mystical imperative game.' Himmler, under Hitler's orders, was searching from France to Tibet for the Holy Grail and similar relics. They were deciphering ancient Germanic runes to their satisfaction to prove that true Germans were Aryans descended from god-men of ancient times. Himmler was creating an entire religion to justify the legitimacy of the criminal thugs who now controlled Germany and were looking hungrily at the rest of the world. To Himmler, the brothers of the Council possessed that secret knowledge which empowered the elect superior few who were entitled to rule the world. Thus, no courtesy or favor was too great for them.

As if not to be outdone, and still pondering the visitor's use of the word 'beloved', the Abbot produced an envelope from the center desk drawer and handed it across the desk to the man. "This is a letter of safe passage, signed by the Patriarch of Constantinople."

"My thanks, Father, we will be crossing to Turkey en route."

"I ask again, is this trip necessary?"

"Father, please. Already the look of starvation is on the land.

The Axis has stripped the country of all food stocks in order to feed the Eastern Front. In addition, this is predicted to be the coldest winter in Russia in the past one hundred years. Once the Nazi beast begins to starve, it will turn its wrath on everything in sight and what they don't devour the communists in the hills are waiting to consume. There may even be an Allied invasion of Greece, complete with bombings, if Churchill has his way." Having made his case, the visitor leaned back in his chair.

"It is good that I am an old man," remarked the Abbot. "You will leave in the morning?"

"If that is possible."

"It will be necessary and wise to take both his tutor and physician."

"Certainly. They will be helpful, as I have come alone."

"Then I will inform them. Will they be traveling to America or returning here?"

"Neither," answered the visitor.

The Abbot, too, sat back and reflected on how simply and delicately the subject of murder had just been dealt with.

CHAPTER SEVENTEEN

October 7
The Cloisters, Fort Tryon Park
New York City

The last time he met with these people, it was in that weird room that they had in the Trump Towers. It was there they had given him the briefcase of money. He had wanted to walk out on them then and there but the money had stopped him. Well, if these nuts wanted him and his people to keep going, they had better ante up some more. 'Assholes,' he thought. At least he was only meeting with one of them today, that head guy, Whiting, probably. Thinking about it, he realized that Whiting had been the only one who mentioned his name. He was glad that he didn't have to go back to that weird room but this place was just as creepy. It was then that he saw Whiting sitting on a stone bench. He walked over and sat down next to him.

"How nice of you to meet me here."

"Look fella, you pay the bills so I meet you where you say. But you and your friends hang out in some strange places."

"Strange, perhaps, but peaceful. Have you never been to The Cloisters before?"

"No. I was raised in New York but never made it here."

"How unfortunate. The Metropolitan Museum of Art went throughout Europe saving segments of religious buildings and bringing them here to make a sort of composite medieval monastery."

"I know; I read the sign coming in. Can we get down to business?"

"I suppose. And where is, as you put it, your number two man?"

"Out in the car, in the parking lot."

"Good."

"Look, I want to talk about money."

"In a moment we can deal with rewards but now let us address the recent problem."

'Hell,' he thought, 'we screw up and they talk about problems and rewards - assholes, real assholes.'

"We were most generous in overlooking your failure to anticipate the whore's ability to defend herself and, thus, the subsequent failure to obtain what we desired from her residence. I had thought we made it clear that we would countenance no more ineptitudes. But it seems that four people slipped away in this town of New Paltz and then another fiasco again at the whore's apartment. That last event even cost us two of our most prized dogs."

"Okay, okay, but we have a way that, within a few hours, a day at the most, we'll find them again so there's no problem."

"No problem? I suppose not. Here, do join me," said the Council member as he pulled a bakery bag from the canvas carry-all at his feet. "I like to come here, it seems so secluded, so quiet; it is hard to believe that you are still in New York City, particularly mid-week when so few come here." With that, he took two sesame honey cakes from the bag, offering one to the hireling as he daintily bit into the other. Simply to pacify his employer, the man impatiently took the cake and shoved it into his mouth.

"It tastes like almonds," he mumbled, crumbs falling from his open mouth.

"How poetic," came the reply as the Council member stood up, "the taste of almond is your reward for failure."

In a moment of realization and panic, he spit out the remainder of the cake but was quite dead before he could say, "Asshole," again.

The man with the canvas carry-all quietly walked through the museum room and out of the gate, wondering if the founder had tasted almond that night so long ago when he was poisoned.

'Oh, well,' he thought, 'time to promote number two, I guess, I do hope he shows more talent than the late, so-called Major.'

PART IV

THE GAME

"Come, Watson, the Game's Afoot."

The Return of Sherlock Holmes
Sir Arthur Conan Doyle

CHAPTER EIGHTEEN

October 6
Sumpter House
Woodstock

Jeanette had breakfast with Howie and me on the veranda. The preparation of epicurean masterpieces was evidently an obsession with our host, Bruce. With great conviction, Jeanette declared, "Bruce feeds our bodies but this view feeds our very souls. Praise the Lord."

"Now down to business," she continued. "Based on what I have already decoded and translated, combined with your background information, taking into consideration current events, here's the most logical general scenario as I see it."

She took a sip of coffee before continuing. Suddenly, with great clarity it dawned on me that all of us had skills, talents, and training that, once we left the intelligence world, were all but useless - a lifetime of experience that had no practical application in the real world. Sure, Jeanette had been ordained and I played at selling antiques but we were shadows, ghosts that didn't know enough to stay in the grave. Howie tried, with moderate success, to bridge the two worlds but I think he realized that he didn't belong in either. That's what allowed him to play fast and loose with the money he came across. In any case, today Jeanette seemed more alive than I had seen her in years. I was glad for that, whatever the reason.

"Jake; are you listening, Jake?" I heard her say.

"Sorry. Just tripping for a minute."

"Well, anyway, the way I see it," Jeanette said, "is that a non-government group based in the U.S. with European origins is planning some kind of indirect power play in Russia very soon. Their front man is someone code-named, "The Pretty Boy." These players apparently have great financial resources and are probably well-connected both here and abroad. Lastly, there appears to be some dissention someplace, maybe within their own ranks, or maybe with some U.S. and/or foreign intelligence agency that may or may not support their operation. But I stress the basic operation is private.

Pleased with her briefing, she sat back in her chair. Howie nodded in earnest approval then spoke, "We checked the phone number in that guy's wallet. It goes to a pay phone in a Stewart's convenience store in some small town way upstate - Cambridge, New York. Jake and I are going to take a run up there this morning."

"Keep me posted. I'll watch the fort here and keep an eye on the girls."

"Shall we?" said Howie. With that we left and headed north.

****

We got to Cambridge by mid-morning and due to Howie's direct, and I thought ill-advised, approach, we quickly found a Russian Orthodox monastery on the outskirts of town. We parked in the visitor lot and got out.

Howie said, "Can you beat that - a Russky church in upstate New York; who would have thought?"

"I don't know but that was really slick, going into that

Stewart's and asking, 'So where do the Russians hang out?"

"It got us here, didn't it?"

I started to answer but was caught in mid-word.

"You hear that?" Howie spat out. "Dogs."

For a brief moment I contemplated getting back into the car. I suspected Howie did too - I saw him involuntarily rub his injured left arm. Instead we followed the sounds down the gravel paths to the kennels.

"Son of a bitch," Howie thought out loud.

"Hey Howie, look," I motioned him over to the display board that had pictures of the dog trained for Solzhenitsyn.

"Yeah, and there's a 2:00 PM exhibition daily of trained dogs."

"I think I'll attend," I said.

"Okay. I'm going to take care of a few things and look around town."

"We only have one car," I reminded him.

"I'll walk."

I hung around the monastery until just before two o'clock. I was really relieved to see the number of tourists that came to the monastery and its gift shop. It was easy to blend in. Quite a few stayed for the dog show.

The dogs were astonishing. The Navy used a fair number of very well trained dogs for a variety of purposes but nothing like these animals. They were programmed not trained. It was then I realized that their handlers were equally programmed. A goateed man who was apparently in charge watched intently from one side. To the casual observer he watched the dogs but it was clear to me that his interest was in the handlers. As the demonstration began to wind down, I saw Goatee walk away. I took a chance that he was worth following and hustled back to the car. I no sooner had the key in the ignition when I caught sight of Goatee driving out in a late model Range Rover.

I hung back but stayed with him. Goatee only went a couple

of miles, mostly down back roads. He turned up a private drive that went back into the woods. I drove by. The area was resplendent in *Keep Out* signs worded in a variety of ways, just so everybody got the message. I was particularly intrigued by the crudely painted one which read "Dog Bites Stay the Hell Out."

I headed back into town and found Howie contentedly sitting on a park bench smoking his pipe, a paper bag on his lap. He saw me as I slowed down.

"My man," he called out.

I was afraid he was dropping his occasional Irish brogue for Afro-American. Howie trotted over to the car, bag in hand. He got in.

"What's in the bag, Howie?"

"You'll laugh, maybe even get upset."

"What's in the bag, Howie?"

"Something I picked up in case we have to do a surveillance, which I think we're probably going to have to do, if you've got good news for me."

"Maybe. Some Pavlovian-type guy, I think he's a player, was at the dog show. I followed him to a real secluded place outside of town. What's in the bag, Howie?"

Howie opened the brown paper bag and pulled out two toy Fisher-Price Walkie-Talkies; he handed one to me.

"Have you been taking your medication?" I boldly asked.

"I told you you wouldn't like it. I do this all the time."

"I'm sure you do."

A car honked its horn behind me and I realized I was blocking traffic. 'Maybe if I fed him,' I thought.

"Hungry?" I said out loud.

"Yeah. Why don't you pull into that McDonald's up there?"

Over Big Macs he explained to me that traveling around the country, from time to time, he ran into an unexpected need for radios and had found that the Fisher-Price Walkie-Talkies actually worked, at least to some degree. Any place in the country he could duck into a Toys-R-Us or something and pick up a set that, in open country, gave him about a quarter mile range. If they managed not to get destroyed, they made good birthday or Christmas gifts for his nieces and nephews. It made sense, which was pretty scary.

Besides toy shopping, Howie also got a room in a no-name motel on a side street just at the end of town.

Over McDonald's coffee, we came up with a plan. If staking out the dog kennel had turned up another location, assuming that I was right that the *Dog Bites Stay the Hell Out* place had some relevance, then it followed that maybe staking out that place might lead us to yet someplace else.

We hung out at the motel until it started getting dark and then headed out to do our surveillance.

Howie, with his trusty Fisher-Price radio, took to the woods across the road from the *Dog Bites* drive-way. I waited out of sight on a dirt road a few hundred yards away. Amazingly, the radios worked, at least after a fashion. I wondered if maybe we could do an ad: "When on stake-out, my partner and I rely on Fisher-Price."

I was dozing off when Howie's voice came out of my toy radio. "Hey Jake, that's it. A beat-up Ford Escort came out headed for town. Take him."

I hit the ignition, it whined but didn't start. 'Damn.' Again; the engine kicked over. With rocks and dirt flying and lights off, I was out onto the road. I almost missed Howie in the dark. Then I saw him waving wildly from the side of the road. I hit the brakes, he jumped in. The tail lights of the Escort went out of sight.

"Better put your lights on," Howie said.

I did as I floored the Chrysler. About a mile down the road there was a red traffic light. One car was between us and the Escort.

We followed it to the Stewart's. He pulled in and parked and a youngish man got out and went to the pay phone inside.

Howie said, "You take the tail light." He got out and trotted to the far corner of the parking lot and started screaming, "You bitch, I don't care if you don't come back. Bitch. Bitch. Bitch."

Meanwhile, with everyone turned towards Howie, I slipped over and put a crack in one of the Escort's plastic tail lights and got back to our car. Following a broken tail light at night is like following a car with a flag on it. Howie doubled back to me and got into the car. He was out of breath.

"Good work, my man."

I overlooked the remark adding, "I think this is the employees' telephone from the *Dog Bites* place."

Just then the Escort's driver came back and got into his car. He was between twenty-five and thirty years old, wearing jeans, black sweatshirt and green jungle combat boots. It was easy to tail him to his next stop - The Dew Drop Inn.

"Can you believe that?" Howie said with real disbelief. "There are still bars named that."

"Maybe it's a joke name, a parody," I suggested.

"Sadly not," he replied.

After a while, I went in and had a beer at the bar, went to the men's room and came out and got back into the car.

"He's in there shooting pool and drinking beer."

"That's a real shit-kicker place; think he's a local boy?"

"Doesn't look that way," I answered.

"Okay, back me up."

"Right," I said with great mental reservation.

It was a little while after midnight when he came out. He came out alone and went directly to his car. In a flash, Howie was behind him.

"My man, my man," Howie called out. Howie was next to him, I was close behind, close enough to see Howie thrust his gun into his stomach.

"Do what I tell you or you're dead."

"Okay, okay."

"Don't shoot him." I was sincerely afraid he might.

"Get in the car over there or I swear I'll kill you." Howie pulled him by the arm back to our car, gun firmly in his stomach.

"Okay, okay. Don't shoot."

Howie shoved him into the back seat and got in with him. I automatically got in and started driving.

"What do you guys want?"

"Shut up," Howie commanded. "Drive to the motel."

We pulled into the motel parking lot and looked around. No one was there. Howie said, "We're going into that room over there and I don't want even the hint of trouble."

The captive was both terrified and revolted.

"Look man, please..."

"I'll kill you here," Howie said, pushing his gun further into the prisoner's stomach. Without further conversation, we made our way to the motel room.

Once inside, Howie threw our captive face first up against the wall. "You know the drill," he said, sounding more than a little crazy, which in fact he probably was. Bending down, he said, "Move and I'll cripple you," as he jammed his pistol into the back of the young man's left knee.

'Dear God,' I thought, 'not again.'

"Howie, don't," I blurted.

His free hand ran expertly over the captive's body. "He's clean," Howie announced, ignoring my comment. With that he grabbed the man by the back of the neck and, spinning him around, thrust him into an armless, straight-back chair. Howie's moves were fast and seemed spontaneous but he was good, very good; every action, every word, were thought out and had a purpose.

Maybe it was because I had been feeling my age in the months before my retirement, but our captive looked young. 'Not much more than a kid,' I thought, 'and a scared kid, at that.'

Scared or not, he had nerve. Pulling himself together, he said in as demanding a voice as he could muster, "Who the hell are you people? This is kidnaping; you can go to jail for this, you know."

"Son, this isn't kidnaping," answered Howie.

"What would you call it?" he spluttered.

"Well," Howie said, taking a seat on the bed opposite him, "I prefer to think of it as effecting custody without the clear color of legal authority."

Sensing weakness in the semantics of Howie's answer, he took the offensive. "You two are going to jail for this and I'm leaving now." He started to get up.

"Sit down, pilgrim," Howie said, leveling his pistol at the center of the kid's chest. The kid slumped back into the chair.

"If anyone's going to jail, my young friend, it's you. Do you think my partner and I brought you here to dress you up like Little Bo Peep and have our way with you or something?" Not getting a reply, Howie shouted, "Well, do you?"

"No, no, I guess not."

Putting a little chuckle in my voice I added, "No, you hope not." After a moment, Howie said, sounding frustrated, "Answer him."

"Right," he said. "I mean, no, no I hope not. Who are you guys? What do you want?" The kid sounded desperate.

"What's your name?" I asked.

"Steve."

"Steve What?"

"Steve Richards, but that's all I'm saying. I want to make a phone call."

"Steve," Howie said, ignoring his request, "Steve, did you go to your high school prom?"

"What?"

"DID...YOU...GO...TO...YOUR...HIGH...SCHOOL...PROM?"
Howie asked very slowly. Turning to me, Howie asked, "That was a simple question, Jake; wasn't it?"

"I think so, but maybe Steve didn't go to high school," I said, attempting to force an affirmative response. I was interested to see that Howie used the Prom Story. I hadn't heard it for a while. On some people, it was really effective; it distracted the subject while simultaneously conjuring up a whole collection of memory-invoked emotions. It allowed the person to view the present crisis from the safe distance of a point in the future.

"Did you go to high school, Steve?" Howie asked.

"Yes," Steve said hesitantly, starting to get confused.

'Who wouldn't?' I thought.

"Well, did you go to your prom?"

"Yeah, sure, sure I went to my prom." We were getting Steve to answer us without him realizing it.

"Good," said Howie. "In the months before the big night, in the weeks, in the days before the prom didn't it seem like it was the most important event in your whole life, like your entire four years at high school were leading up to the night of the prom? Getting a date, asking the right girl, being afraid that she'd turn you down, the possibility of not going because you didn't have a date, you know, the whole nine yards. Remember that?"

"Yeah, yeah I remember," he answered again.

"The night of your prom wasn't it the most important night of your whole life?"

"Yeah, I guess it was, sure," Steve said, bewildered at where this was going.

After a long pause, Howie leaned over and, putting his hand on Steve's leg, said quietly, "Steve, what does your prom mean to you now," he paused," right now, tonight?"

"Not much; nothing at all, really," came the answer.

"That's right," Howie said, "and right now you must feel that tonight is the worst night of your life." Howie paused for an answer.

"Pretty close."

"Well, a week from now, well more like a year from now, you'll look back on tonight like you do your prom. It will be just a memory, a bad one maybe, but a memory just the same." Howie was quiet for a long time and then continued. "That's if you handle everything right tonight."

"You want to handle everything right, don't you Steve," I said, "so that tonight becomes just a memory?" minimizing the reality of the situation.

"I'm not saying anything."

'Sure you are,' I thought, 'but you just don't realize it and we're barely getting started.'

Howie leaned back and holstered his gun under his jacket, then began again.

"First, let me tell you, officially inform you, which is our duty, actually to warn you that you are not allowed to give us any information so we are not going to ask you any questions and I don't want you to tell us anything. I repeat, under no circumstances are you to volunteer information. Is that clear?"

"Is that clear?" repeated Howie, raising his voice slightly.

"Yes, yeah sure, that's clear."

"Good," Howie answered tersely, "now, since we're not going the Little Bo Peep route, we obviously didn't just grab you at random. So, if we didn't grab you at random, then we planned to pick you up. Obviously, we had this all worked out because we knew where you were and when, or about when, you'd get there and we had this motel room ready to bring you here. So, it was pretty well planned and that means we know a lot about you and your friends. You follow me?"

"Yeah, I guess so."

"Okay. I'm not going to say we know everything about you but we know eighty, maybe eighty-five percent of the story."

"So, what do you want from me?"

"We want to give you the test and if you pass the test then you will automatically be on the right road again."

"I have no idea what you are talking about. Besides, if you know so much, how come you had to ask my name?"

"That was part of the test," I said.

"Right," said Howie, "and there was the screw up with the high altitude infrared surveillance tapes. Still shots of you were taken from them and faxed to us and with infrared, the positive becomes the negative and the negative becomes the positive when you fax them. So, at first, we thought you were a black guy but that's beside the point. Explain the test to him, Jake."

"Okay. Here's how it works. You tell us something we already know and since we already know it then we know you are being honest with us and we can trust you to come back on the right road which you took the wrong fork off of."

"Right," added Howie, "you took the wrong fork."

As if briefly contemplating a proposal, Howie stopped then pressed ahead with renewed vigor. "Then," he said, "then besides giving us information we already know, you are going to be required to provide a legal proof of your sincerity."

Melding into Howie's rhythm, I added, "Normally, that legal proof would be simply a signed statement but here it will be necessary to actually assist us in the next few days."

"I think both of you are crazy. I have no idea what you're talking about, besides you don't know who I work for."

"I wouldn't push the 'crazy' thing too far, if I were you," I said.

"I bet you're going to tell us you work for CIA or something, right?" Howie said.

"Maybe," answered Steve, trying to sound enigmatic.

"Steve, let me tell you something," I said, " CIA, none of the intelligence services, recruit out of *Soldier of Fortune*." To underscore my authority, I handed him my old Naval Investigative Service ID, complete with gold-anchor-embossed leather case.

Howie quickly flashed something which could as easily have been his Connecticut driver's license as anything else.

"Okay, so you guys are legit. So check me out. I'm working for the company."

"The only company you're working for is bad company," I said, putting a fair amount of disgust in my voice.

Howie, sounding more friendly, said, "Look, Steve, do you remember a couple of years ago some former American G.I. answered an ad in *Soldier of Fortune* magazine and went to work for the Englishman, Mad Mike, in Angola about the time Mad Mike's operation was falling apart?"

"You mean the guy that got shot?"

"Not just shot, executed - put in front of a firing squad."

Then I added, "How about the guy who put an ad in the magazine down in Texas? He wanted to be a mercenary so bad he wound up murdering some guy's wife for a couple of grand. You know that story?"

"He's the one that got executed."

"Beginning to see a pattern here?" Howie asked.

"Look," I said, "I'll give you one more. There was a contract guy who actually did work for CIA for a while but his contract didn't get renewed, so he goes to work for Khadafy and tells some of his old buddies that he's undercover for, as you put it, "The Company." He tries to recruit a couple of them and for a while his story works, then someone gets suspicious and, bang, now he's doing life in super max."

"That's that underground Federal Prison; it's sort of like being buried alive," Howie added.

"But these guys who recruited us are loaded, money's no object. They're well-connected and have big plans, I mean BIG plans," Steve offered.

"So do Columbian drug dealers," I said.

"I got nothing to say," Steve spat, taking his last stand.

"John said you're a stand-up guy," Howie flattered, bluffing with the name of the now-crippled dog handler from Françoise's apartment. It was a safe bluff. Seeing a glimmer of recognition in Steve's eyes told us it was a good one.

"You know John." I said.

"John Who?"

"John Fredericks," Howie answered impatiently. "Look, Steve," he continued, "don't test us, we're testing you."

"We don't have much time," I said. "Your window of opportunity is closing. We didn't just pull John's name out of the air, and we didn't pick you up at random. We can prove who we work for. You, on the other hand, got your job through some arm-chair adventurers' magazine that anybody can advertise in. Look, you've got to know we know the whole story, or at least most of it." At this point, Steve had to believe that we did.

"I want to talk to John," Steve demanded.

"Should we tell him?" I asked.

"Why not? I want to save this kid... and so did John," Howie paused; I knew he was trying to think of what to say next. "Steve," he continued, " John's dead...his dying words were about you, to get you out of this mess. I'm sorry, Steve." Howie hung his head.

'That was good,' I thought. I hadn't expected it but it was working.

Howie stood up and put his hand on Steve's shoulder, "Go on," he said, "tell us about it."

Howie was going for the kill but it was premature.

"What happened? How did it happen?"

"They," Howie started, emphasizing the word they, "they killed him. We got there too late, but it's not too late for you."

"Why? Why did they do it?" Steve's body language betrayed him. The shock of believing that John was dead was beginning to crack him.

"He found out about them and confronted them," Howie pushed on. Howie was doing great but I was hoping he could keep straight what was fact and what was his fiction spun for Steve's benefit. The art of sophisticated interrogation always fascinated me. Anyone could beat or coerce a confession from someone but only a few unique individuals could use seemingly innocuous anecdotes mixed with fabrications and guesses to psychologically manipulate a person so completely.

"Is he really dead?" Steve asked, not really expecting an answer, then continued, "I had some suspicions about these guys, too."

'We're almost there,' I thought. Steve was "me-tooing" to what he thought his friend had done. He also, without consciously realizing it, had used the past tense. Howie was silent, obviously trying to find the key to push him over the brink.

Steve began to speak again. "I still don't know if I should trust you guys," he said, "I don't understand why you'd need me to tell you anything if you know it all already. Why don't you just tell me what you know?"

"The other day, Steve, I was taking a nap on my sister's couch," Howie started...

'The Dollar Bill Story,' I thought, 'a real classic interrogation routine.'

"There I was, almost asleep and I see my little nephew take a ten dollar bill out of my wallet. I didn't say anything for a couple of hours then I asked him about it and he kind of looked down at the ground and said, 'Yeah, Uncle Howie, here's what I've got left. I spent the rest.' Steve, how would you feel if that happened to you?"

"I'd be pretty mad at the kid, I guess," said Steve, shifting in his chair, showing some impatience that we had drifted off into trivialities again.

"How would you feel in the same situation," Howie said, "if the kid looked you straight in the eye and said, 'I don't know what you're talking about.'?" Not waiting for an answer, Howie continued, "Everybody makes mistakes but what is important is whether or not a man," Howie emphasized the word man, "can tell the truth when the time comes. We need you to tell us the truth about this situation and about yourself. We want to be able to trust you."

"Trust? I don't know who to trust any more, except myself. If you want to arrest me, lock me up, go ahead but I'm not going to rat on anybody."

Howie thought for a moment and pulled out his wallet and took out a folded up Xerox of a newspaper picture with a caption. "See this picture, Steve? I found it the other day while I was doing research on something. It's from the old New York Daily Mirror back in 1945. You can see for yourself it's a Japanese soldier helping to navigate a flight of Mitchell Bombers on a raid over Japan. I bet you thought that Japanese soldiers were real fanatics that fought to the death or killed themselves or something, never surrender - let alone switch sides."

Steve examined the clipping with interest.

"Steve," I said, "a rat is somebody who turns on his friends to save himself. I think what Howie is trying to tell you is that there is nothing dishonorable in doing the right thing and changing sides once you find out you've been lied to and conned and are working for the wrong people."

"Yeah," said Howie, "this Jap soldier, and a lot of others, finally woke up and realized that the Emperor wasn't God, that they had started the war, that they were losing the war, and that a lot of Japanese civilians were dying because they were being lied to. Now Steve, I want you to tell us about yourself." Howie was going for the kill again.

"Start by telling us about John - how long you've known him, where you met..." I said, pushing and directing him a little further.

"John and I grew up together; we lived next door to each other for twenty-three years. He had a job and was engaged. It's my fault."

"Fault doesn't matter now," Howie said. "What matters now is that you do the right thing, make things right...for your sake and for John's sake. We have to know if we can really trust you, Steve. Tell us all about yourself now."

"In school, John was the popular one, I never made or was picked for any team. I was the guy without a car, without a date; I was a nobody. My folks didn't have the money or desire to send me to college. I wanted to go to West Point but couldn't get in. I joined the Army and made it into Rotory Flight School, I was going to be a chopper pilot and a warrant officer. Right at the end of flight school, just before Desert Storm, they find out I've got asthma and they kick me out. I grew up on fishing boats and I could fly choppers but had no license, no job. Then..."

"Then you see this ad for the Southern Cross Corporation in good, old *Soldier of Fortune*," Howie said.

"Yeah, I saw a ticket out of Gulf Breeze, Florida, so I talk John into checking it out with me. He wanted to make some extra money because, like I said, he was getting married and he had spent a couple of years in the Marine Corps."

"Okay, Steve, what was your rôle in all of this?"

"I was hired as a chopper pilot and a boat hand. I was perfect for the job. The people we worked for are bringing a boat, a yacht, up the river, the Hudson, tomorrow. The name of the yacht is the *Reindeer*. It's a big boat; I've been on it. It's a twin to the yacht that Forbes used to own. You know, the one that sits in the East River in the City with the small bell helicopter on the aft deck. Tomorrow night, some time after midnight, I'm to pick up a Zodiac boat in a yard on the river south of here, rendezvous with the yacht at first light, take the chopper to the estate on the other side of town and pick up a couple of passengers, one of which is a guy they're going to insert into Russia in some kind of power play. That's one of the reasons I believed they were the CIA. Who else would try to pull off something like that and have the money to do it?"

"How about the Russian Mafia?" Howie asked.

"I didn't think about that. I guess I didn't think about much. For the first time I was a player, a part of something, something big."

"Well, you're on the right team now," I said. He looked skeptical.

"You were close to John, weren't you?" Howie asked.

"We were like brothers, maybe closer. I'm so sorry for getting him involved."

"Do you want to go to prison or do you really want to work for the government...Do you want to get them back, get them back for John?" It was a rhetorical question.

"Please," was all he said as he completely broke down.

****

Howie and I stepped outside the door into the crisp, fresh night air. The sky was clear with bright stars. I hesitated a moment before completely closing the door. I thought about it. He was no threat, we had broken him. I closed the door. No, he wasn't any threat, we had broken and rebuilt him. He was ours now.

I lit a cigarette and offered one to Howie. He took it.

Nice interrogation," I said quietly.

"You did pretty good yourself," he said. "We work well together."

Howie looked tired. The interrogation and the events of the past few days combined to drain him. I was wasted, too.

"His story makes sense," Howie said.

"It's coming together. We're close, Howie. You carry that old Jap photo with you; is it real?"

"Yeah, well, it's a Xerox. I got the original at home."

"I find it hard to believe that any of the Emperor's devotees could be merely talked or coerced into switching sides simply because someone showed them the error of their ways."

"What happened was some O.S.S. guy finally realized that the Japanese sense of community, of being a part of a community, is what their fanatical loyalty was largely based on. Take one of them out of that community physically, and more importantly psychologically, and they couldn't stand it. It was worse than death itself. Isolate them and they sought a new community, even if the new one was actually an old enemy."

"Interesting," I said. It really was.

"Let's get some sleep." Howie said, crushing out his cigarette and turning to the door.

"Wait, do you want to post a watch?"

"Nah, he's okay. Besides, I always sleep with one eye open."

I bet he did, at that.

CHAPTER NINETEEN

October 7
No-Name Motel
Cambridge

I woke up about 7:00 AM. Our new recruit was sleeping like a babe. Howie stared at me through one open eye from the chair he had slept in. Weird.

I went out to get some badly needed coffee and find a pay phone.

"Good morning, Sumpter House. How may I help you?" answered an effeminate male voice.

"This is Jake O'Brien. Let me speak to Jeanette."

"Please hold, sir. I'll see if the Reverend Quinlan is available." I was put on hold and, after what seemed to be an eternity, I heard Jeanette's voice.

"Jake. Jake, is that you?"

"Yeah, it's me. What's up?"

"Are you okay? Where are you?" She seemed controlled but obviously stressed.

"Up in Cambridge. What's going on?"

"Everything's okay now, but we got hit last night."

"What do you mean? Is...?"

"Rachel's okay. They never made it to the house."

"Jeanette.."

"Just listen, Jake." She paused then continued. "About 3:00 A.M., a dozen or so, maybe more, probably more, G.I. Joe types came up the mountain. My God, they never had a chance between the perimeter alarms, the booby traps and Bruce's people. We were on them before they knew what happened. It was over in minutes."

"What the hell happened?"

"There was some shooting. We're okay but, look, they took casualties - a couple dead, some wounded, and we took three prisoners.

"Prisoners! Christ it sounds like Vietnam."

"You would have had a real sense of deja vu."

"Are you sure Rachel is safe?"

"She's okay. So's Françoise. Don't worry, we hurt them pretty bad. They didn't expect it and now they know they've lost the element of surprise. Bruce brought in some reinforcements and he also had some Woodstock cops in already this morning. I think they're on the payroll. Bruce's guys are efficient. Within half an hour this place was completely cleaned up. Amazing."

I was beginning to think you could do anything you wanted in this country anymore as long as you cleaned up afterwards. I didn't have the heart to ask what they did with the bodies. Remembering how I got into this in the first place, I figured they probably called the NYPD to come and dress them up and claim that they all died of heart failure.

"Look, Jake," Jeanette said, interrupting my thoughts, "I've got some information for you."

"Wait a minute," I said. "How did they find you?" I could feel the paranoia flooding over me.

"That's one of the things I want to tell you. Do you still

146

have that car you brought up from the City?"

"Yeah."

"Well, get rid of it. It's got some kind of tracking device on it with a range of about three to five miles. They made a calculated guess that you probably headed for the New Paltz area and..."

"They cruised around 'til they found it. But then they knew I wasn't there when they hit you."

"It was Rachel they were after."

"Jesus."

"They were looking for the papers you gave me. They figured if they snatched Rachel up they could make an exchange and neutralize you as well."

"How did you manage to come to that conclusion?" I asked, feeling like I was in some kind of bad dream.

"Bruce's guys did... well, a fast field interrogation on the ones we took."

"Interrogation?"

"If you want to call it that. Does the love scene from the movie, *Deliverance*, mean anything to you?"

"Oh no," I heard come out of my mouth. "Did they...?"

"Make them squeal like pigs? I don't know. I went for a walk."

"Look," she went on, " these guys, for the most part were wannabes who thought they were working for CIA, which you and I know is total nonsense. The people running this are definitely private free-lancers doing their own thing. But don't underestimate them; they've got money, resources, connections and big plans, real big."

"That's the feeling we got up here."

"Well, stay there and wrap this up. We're okay here."

"Okay," I paused. "What else do you have?"

"Bruce and I broke the codes. It hit me suddenly. I was going about it all wrong. It wasn't a progression system..." she started.

"Skip the technical stuff," I interrupted, "What's it say?"

"It's a list of contacts, supporters, compromised individuals, maybe allies, all kinds of people they're connected with in high and, I guess, low places."

"Like where?"

"U.S. Department of State, Russian Foreign Service, former KGB types, heavy contacts in all the Russian parties - Nationalist, Communist, Royalist, etc. - contacts in the Russian Mafia, some business and industrial leaders in the U.S. and Europe, oh, and a lot of media folks here and over there."

' "What's the plan as you see it?"

"These people have some guy they call The Pretty Boy, whatever's the story with him, but they're making a move to put him in power in Russia. Well, not exactly - it's not a coup in the traditional sense but nonetheless they're making some kind of power play with him in the next couple of days.

"Maybe, maybe not," I said, trying to sound enigmatic.

"One more thing, Jake. Whoever is the government boss on our side, he'd better get here. It's time to bring them in."

"Right. Will do. Take care of yourself."

"You too, Jake."

I went back to the motel room. Our new-found friend was in the shower. Howie was watching CNN. He left the T.V. and sipped the coffee I had brought him as I recounted my conversation with Jeanette.

His only comment came during Jeanette's description of the "Field Interrogation." "Wow," he exclaimed, "The Reverend is going to have to take a Minister's Refresher Course after this!"

"Howie," I urged, "I think you should call any and all of your contacts in Washington who might be interested in this and let them know what's happening."

He didn't answer verbally but nodded his head in agreement and said, "I'm not going to give them the details but I will tell them we're taking the boat tonight."

****

There were several vacant seats around the great wooden council table. Those members present were engaged in hot debate.

"I was always against hiring these people on ethical grounds but that argument pales in comparison to their incompetence."

"Admittedly, they have been less than successful," came one reply.

"Less than successful? They actually engaged in a battle last night and LOST. This is absurd!" another man exclaimed.

The man at the head of the table ended the debate. "No matter now. In any case, they have occupied and misdirected our adversaries, and now it is too late for them. Let us adjourn and move to our respective positions in the field. Each of us knows his assignment."

CHAPTER TWENTY

October 7
Cambridge

Howie went to the main street and found a couple of locals who jumped at the offer of a thousand dollars in travelers checks to drive his "Mother's" car to Boston. From there he walked next door to the Frugal Car Rental Agency and rented us an unidentifiable older model four door.

Meanwhile, with our new recruit Steve, I located a sporting goods store and purchased a 12 gauge Mossberg pump shotgun and a model 700 Remington rifle chambered in .308 along with a fair amount of ammunition for both. I was never an advocate for gun control but being able to outfit yourself over the counter for a coming gunfight was ridiculous. The military version of the Remington 700 was what the Army and Marine Corps used as a sniper rifle so I figured it was good enough for us.

Assuming that we were stocking up for the approaching hunting season, we were asked by the proprietor to sign a petition/pledge to "Keep Our Woods Litter Free." I assured him that we were very tidy and always cleaned up after shooting events. He seemed pleased.

Howie met us for lunch at the local McDonald's. It seemed a bit Kafka-esque to be eating Big Macs and fries, while planning to hijack a yacht in a few hours, when only feet away, kids were consuming Happy Meals in the play land under their mothers' watchful eyes.

After lunch, we sent Steve on a mission back to the motel room to saw down the barrel of the shotgun. Howie was obsessed that he cut it no shorter than 16 inches, not wanting to violate the Federal law on illegal weapons. It seemed kind of strange under the circumstances, particularly coming from a man who had recently shot someone in the knee with very little provocation. Stranger still was that I understood and agreed with his thought process.

While Steve was measuring and sawing away, Howie and I sat on a bench in the park-like courtyard of the motel. It was hard not to be affected by the warm sun which cut through the cool, crisp autumn air. The turning leaves were at their peak and were truly magnificent. The breeze was beginning to blow the weaker ones from the trees and across the ground - an ominous sign amidst the tranquility and beauty.

Howie took his burning pipe from his mouth and, looking straight ahead, said, "So, Jake, you got a plan?"

"Not really," I answered, then quickly added, "But one thing's real clear."

"Yeah? What's that?"

"All three of us can't row up to the boat tonight."

"Right. They're expecting Steve and only Steve."

"Yeah, and we both trust Steve, but not completely. Right?"

"No, not completely," I said. "But as I see it, we've got no other choice."

"Okay, Jake. So, Steve goes out to meet this boat. What's its name again?"

"*Reindeer.*"

"Right. And he gets on it and goes to see the boss man. He holds him hostage, signals us and we come on board."

"That's the plan, I guess. It's dicey but I think that he can carry it off," I commented.

"And dicier still that he doesn't betray us."

"Right."

"Downside," Howie stated officially.

"He doesn't pull it off and we don't get the signal to board," I answered.

"So, their plan gets screwed up without their chopper pilot, giving us time to call in the cavalry from Washington."

"Okay," I stuck in, "or he doesn't pull it off but does signal us or signals us because he's switched sides again."

"Then we buy the farm when we board the boat and some-one else is going to have to keep America safe for democracy."

There was no need for further conversation.

We spent the rest of the afternoon and evening just hanging out, mostly in the motel room, trying to get some sleep, check-ing the weapons, turning the TV on for a while and surfing through the channels before flipping it off. Howie spent time reading a paperback spy novel while Steve played solitaire with a well-worn deck of cards he carried in his jacket pocket. He was an emotional loner. All of us did what we could to ignore and deny the growing tension.

Finally, a little after midnight, Howie woke up from a nap, looked at his watch and said, "Okay, let's do it." The tension instantly evaporated as adrenalin pumped into our systems.

I sat in the back seat as we drove over extremely dark coun-try roads. The trip took about 45 minutes. The entire way, we took turns reviewing, in sequence and out loud, our rôles in the operation.

The boat yard, a few miles south of Troy, didn't amount to much, which is what I expected. No one was around; there was no night watchman. The most impressive craft there was Steve's Zodiac. I helped Steve make it ready while Howie looked for a small dinghy with a good outboard motor for us to steal.

We worked fast and in a few minutes were ready to shove

off. Howie gave Steve a last minute pep talk.

"Okay, when we get near the *Reindeer*, Jake and I will fall back 50 yards or so. It's dark enough tonight so they won't see us at that distance. The Zodiac engine noise will drown out our engine. When you signal us with the flashlight, we'll come in but you should have everything under control by then.

"Don't worry," Steve said with a lot more confidence and resolve than Howie and I had at that point. Steve slung the Kalashnikov over his back and jammed a three-cell mag light into his belt. We headed south down the Hudson. The night seemed cold as hell.

About fifteen miles downstream, just south of the Catskill Bridge, we caught sight of the yacht *Reindeer*. We cut our engine and bobbed in the wake of the Zodiac as it pulled ahead like a torpedo aimed straight for the yacht's mid-section. A few yards out, Steve cut his engine and swung gracefully into the harsh electric light that encapsuled the yacht. As precisely as a toy on a track, the Zodiac stopped at the foot of a gangway leading up to the deck. We could see two or three men waiting at the top of the gangway, one hung over the rail assisting in some way with the mooring of the Zodiac. After a couple of minutes, Steve climbed the stairs and went with the waiting men up to the bridge and disappeared inside its warm glow.

Time in our little dinghy passed, and passed as if we were in some cold, all-enveloping, dark, sensory deprivation tank. Only the occasional breeze and the rhythmic lapping of the water against the sides gave us any sense of reality.

Finally a blinking light. Without a word, Howie pulled the outboard motor on and we lurched forward. It seemed that I only had time to grab the shotgun and position myself before Howie wedged the dinghy between the Zodiac and the gangway. I swung out onto the steps of the gangway and attempted to steady the dinghy. Howie stood up and, with surprising dexterity, literally ran out of the small boat. Stepping on my back, he ran up the steps, carrying the Remington rifle. He showed such determination that I was convinced he could have crossed a short distance on water. I followed him up the gangway.

Reaching the top, we scanned the deck. No one. Without a word, we headed for the bridge. We got there and Howie, back to the wall, covered me as I kicked in the door. He followed me through. The bridge was empty. Light came up through a door at the base of a small flight of stairs at the rear of the bridge cabin.

"Down here, guys." It was Steve's familiar voice.

Howie laid the rifle down quietly and took out his pistol. We went down the stairs carefully, very carefully.

I can't say we burst into the room, it was more like we slithered. Howie to the left, me to the right.

We found ourselves in the luxurious salon of the yacht. Lying neatly on the floor lined up like pencils were the six crew members. Each had his hands folded behind his neck. Sitting almost casually in a leather chair was a well-dressed, older man. Steve stood with his back to a corner, Kalashnikov leveled dangerously at the room. He seemed almost relaxed, pleased with himself.

"So this is the rest of your band of riff-raff," said the man in the chair disdainfully.

"Riff-raff with guns," Howie said.

"Yeah, and the rest of us will be here soon," I added boldly.

"Really," said the man in the chair. "I think not. I think it's only the three of you."

"That's enough," snapped Howie.

I wasn't sure how he meant that but the man in the chair sat back in bored annoyance.

"Anyone else on board?" I asked Steve.

"I don't think so."

"Okay. Pat these guys down and lock them up someplace."

"Me as well?" the seated man asked with a sneer.

"No. You stay where you are," answered Howie.

"The galley's behind the salon and is steel encased with no windows and a good, lockable door," suggested Steve.

"Okay, get them in there."

"Do you want me to get the knives and stuff like that out of there?" asked Steve.

"Don't bother. If these guys want to stab each other that's okay with me," I said, "so just take a quick look around in there while Howie pats them down." Within a couple of minutes, the six man crew was searched and shut away.

I stayed in the salon while Howie and Steve checked the yacht for anyone else. After a few moments of silence, the seated man said, "Allow me to introduce myself; my name is Carl Whiting. And you are, sir?"

"Jake O'Brien."

"Well, Mr. Jake O'Brien, what do you think happens now?"

I didn't like his choice of words but answered him anyway. "You got me, we're winging this."

"Yes, I rather imagine you are."

Our brief conversation was terminated by the return of Howie and Steve. "The boat is clean. We got 'em all," Howie said. "The kid here," indicating Steve, "did some job. He was telling me about it."

"Well, it wasn't so much," Steve said pridefully understating his success. "It was really very easy. The skipper and the mate met me on deck and brought me up to the salon. I got the drop on all three of them. Then I had the skipper order the other three guys up here and, well, that's all she wrote."

'Got the drop on them,' I thought. Steve's only worldly experience must have come from his TV set but anyway I said, quite truthfully, "Easy or not it could have worked out a lot differently."

"A lot differently," Howie added for emphasis.

Whiting picked up a copy of William Manchester's

MacArthur: An American Caesar and opening it to the bookmark about half way through the tome, began to read to himself, seemingly oblivious to us and his situation.

It was about 5:00 A.M. and we settled down to wait for sunrise, which would be in about an hour or so.

Steve took out his deck of cards and played countless games, lost in his own thoughts, if any. When the first grey light of dawn began to appear outside the salon windows, he simply gathered up the cards and stuck them back in his jacket. "I'm going down to check the chopper," he said.

"I'll go with you," Howie announced, and with that they left.

Whiting put his book down. "You're going to try to bring him here, aren't you?" he said.

"Bring who here?"

"The young one. Don't be coy; you know of whom I speak. Anyway, I need to use the toilet. I suppose you would like to accompany me?"

When we returned to the salon he sat in a different leather chair. Steve came in a few minutes later. "We're all set and ready to go," he said.

"Okay," I answered. "Get going and take care of yourself."

Without fully taking my eyes from Whiting, I watched Steve run back to the helicopter and, looking like old comrades, saw Howie and Steve climb into the machine. Slowly tilting slightly forward, it lifted off the deck. Banking sharply, they circled the yacht twice, then headed due east into the rising sun, gaining altitude as they went.

"So, Mr. O'Brien, we are alone."

"Except for half a dozen people in the galley."

"They are of no consequence, so let us talk."

"About what?"

"Our organization, our purpose, our plans. I think you have some insight into them but it is limited, very limited."

"Limited or not, I think you are about to broaden my horizons, aren't you?"

"In a manner of speaking. Do you know the identity of the person your friends are on their way to get?"

"Some character you and this organization of yours are using to front for you in some lateral power play in Russia. Am I close enough?"

"Close, I believe the colloquial expression is, but no cigar. To begin with, our organization is known as the Council or, more formally, the Council of Twelve. Some non-member intimates refer to us as The Rasputin Club."

"Catchy name," I said. "Is this going someplace?"

"Perhaps. Do sit down and I'll tell you the story. If nothing else, it will pass the time."

I sat down opposite him with the shotgun on my lap. If he wanted to talk, I'd listen.

"Do you know who Rasputin was?" he asked.

"He was some kind of Russian monk. Evidently knew something about hypnosis because he used it to control the bleeding of one of the Tsar's kids who was a hemophiliac. They used to call him the Mad Monk."

"Basically, but it wasn't one of the Tsar's kids, as you put it, it was THE kid, Tsar Nicholas' son, Alexis. Alexis, the Crown Prince, heir to the Romanov Dynasty and throne of all the Russias. Incidentally, were you aware that the title Tsar is derived from Caesar? The name came to be synonymous with the emperors of the Roman Empire and," he said with added emphasis, "the head of the Christian Church after the reign of Constantine. Nicholas followed in that tradition as the last absolute monarch in the world and the official head of one of the largest and most mystical Christian sects. But I digress. Back to Rasputin. Father Rasputin was a Starets, a self-proclaimed or, as I prefer, self-revealed, holy man. It is said he spoke directly to God and God to him."

"Why are you telling me all this?" I asked.

"Perhaps because when you realize who and what we are, and what is about to occur, well, you might elect to abandon your folly and join us.

"Not likely."

"No, it's not but nonetheless, attempt to keep an open mind. But should you remain unconvinced, then you and your friends will not live to leave this river so it won't matter anyway. Now, where was I?"

"Rasputin's talking to God."

"Oh yes. He had great powers. He used those powers in a futile attempt to save Russia and the world from Communism. But that was not in his destiny. However, it was his foresight that saved the heir to the Tsar's family."

"The legendary daughter, Anastasia?"

"No," he laughed. "Anastasia's survival is only a romantic legend. No, Mr. O'Brien, it was Alexis the Crown Prince that he saved. He saved his son."

"Wait a minute. I thought you said he saved the Crown Prince, Nicholas' son."

"This may shock your Irish Catholic morality, Mr. O'Brien, but Alexis was Nicholas' son in name only. Rasputin was Alexis' spiritual and blood father. It was Father Rasputin's seed that was planted in the Empress' womb."

"So the Tsar's wife was sleeping with this crazy, self-made monk," I commented cynically.

"God-made, Mr. O'Brien. Father Rasputin had studied and practiced in the Khlysty sect where sexual abandonment is a necessary element in obtaining spiritual redemption. I sense your skepticism but I am unconcerned with your philosophic opinions."

"So, it's the monk's bastard son who will be returning in the helicopter?"

"Not exactly. Allow me to continue. The young Alexis escaped Russia and was raised in an isolated monastery away from the influences of the world. At the appropriate time, he married for the purpose of continuing the line."

"Who'd he marry?" I thought this should be interesting.

"His half-sister. Father Rasputin's daughter by his first wife."

"Wow," I heard myself saying out loud.

"When a child was born, a man child, Alexis, well, he passed away."

'I bet,' I thought.

"So that's who's coming?" I asked. "The child Alexis fathered by his sister?"

"No. At the appropriate time, there was another marriage."

"Right," I said, "and when a kid was born, the father bought the farm. Sort of like black widow spiders."

"Your metaphors are so colorful but nonetheless accurate."

"Who did he marry?"

"A niece of Tsar Nicholas."

"Wow," I said again.

"I don't expect you to understand and I'm certainly not concerned with your moral judgements. But through these arranged marriages we have produced a legitimate male heir to the Romanovs and to the Russian throne, an heir who also has the spiritual life blood of Father Rasputin. In short, an heir and a messiah."

'Boy, was this guy a loon,' I thought. "I've got to say that a guy this inbred, who's great-grandfather was a nut to begin with, can't be playing with a full deck." I stopped short of asking how many toes he had.

"Your middle-class understandings are quaint, Mr. O'Brien. Arranged family marriages and sibling unions are not uncommon in royal history. For thousands of years, Egyptian Pharaohs wed their sisters. For who else can a god marry but one of his own?"

"Nonetheless," I said, "this guy, god or not, must be, uh, sort of different; I think the politically correct term is special."

"Yes, quite special. The average person such as yourself would not see beyond, shall we say, some obvious unusual features. Did you know that Native Americans believed that insanity was an indication that a person was more spiritually evolved?"

"Well, anyway," I said, "you and your Council expect to put this "special" person back on the throne of Russia just because of his blood line?"

"No, not on the throne but, well, next to it. While it is not difficult to take over a government, it is tedious trying to hold onto it, what with free elections and petty political rivalries."

"Those pesky elections will get you every time," I remarked dryly.

"Exactly. But within each Russian political party, and in each Russian, there is a significant element that would welcome a monarch of some sort, spiritual or secular, off to one side, to advise, unite, stabilize and, above all, give identity to the country. There are also those outside of Russia who would support such a move, as well."

"I got it. Governments and presidents come and go but your guy would stay."

"Precisely, Mr. O'Brien."

"And you and the other eleven guys on your Council make out pretty well when you're running the show from back stage."

"Sadly, some members of the Council are motivated by greed and personal agendas but others are true believers."

"True believers in what?" I asked.

"Believers in pure blood lines. Believers in the truth of the reality that some are born with the right to rule and most are born to serve. Believers in the Divine Right of monarchs. Believers who understand that it is time, it is past the time, to bring those monarchs back to restore order, stability, beauty and romance to the world, or at least a good part of it."

"Okay, okay," I said. "Some of you may believe in this spiritual blood line hocus-pocus but I don't buy that you can sell it to the average man in the street today."

"Really, Mr. O'Brien? Did you know that when the British rescued the Grand Duchess Xenia and brought her to London, that when her servants first saw the English King, George V, they fell to the ground and kissed the hem of his coat, believing him to be the Tsar brought back to life, resurrected."

"That was some seventy years ago."

"Oh, seventy years is a long time, is it, Mr. O'Brien? Maybe in the West but not in the Orient. It would be wise to remember what Kipling said, "Europeans don't understand the Russians because we see them as the most Eastern of the Western people when they are the most Western of the Eastern people.""

"This is really fascinating but while I've got you in such a talkative mood, let me ask you something. Who pays for all of this?"

"The vast majority of the Romanov wealth was kept in discreet banks outside of Russia. Father Rasputin knew how to access all of it. We have wealth beyond belief, Mr. O'Brien; does that interest you?"

"Maybe," I said. "Are you offering me membership on your Council?"

"Hardly. We sit for life and we choose our successors very carefully. It has been that way since the Council was established. But we have many, many people.." Whiting hesitated.

"On your payroll?" I finished for him.

Whiting nodded affirmatively with a smile then leaned forward and said, "Name your price, Mr. O'Brien. If not money, we will fulfill your greatest fantasy."

"I'm tempted, truly I am, but, well, I gotta turn you down."

"More's the pity, Mr. O'Brien. I did tell you, didn't I, that you and your friends will never leave the river alive?"

"Maybe, maybe not, but with you as a hostage, we've got a chance. Besides, I think this heir they're bringing back depends on you. That's why you're the Council member who's here, and I don't think he wants you hurt. No, Mr. Whiting, I think we'll make it off the river and we will meet again when you are in Federal Court."

"You are astute, Mr. O'Brien. I have underestimated you in many ways. Since I don't suppose we can use the galley, do you think you could get us the sealed tin of honey cakes in the cupboard beneath the bar over there?"

"No, you get them and then get back over here and sit down, but you even breathe funny and I'll cut you in half."

"And lose your hostage? I'm only of value to you alive, as you have just pointed out." He moved to the cabinet, got the tin and pulled the cellophane off it, carelessly dropping it on the floor. He sat and, taking the lid off the tin, extended it to me saying, "Have one, they're quite delightful."

I took one with my left hand but dropped it back. "Maybe later," I said.

"Too bad," Whiting said. Taking one, he stuffed it whole into his mouth and bit down. It must have had a lot of cyanide because he was dead almost immediately. Fast but painful. His death throes knocked him out of the chair and onto the floor. I'd seen a few men killed in my life but something about this shocked the hell out of me. I sat stunned in the chair for a while. I guess he was one of the True Believers.

I got up with my shotgun and walked out on deck and lit a cigarette.

Back in Vietnam when I was working the river, I had a sailor on my boat who had been an English major before dropping out of college. He wanted to write the story of the Riverine Force but said no one would ever believe it. Admiral Zumwalt's Riverine Force has to be one of the strangest episodes in the history of the U.S. Navy. He said that the story could only be told as fiction. Years later, in Grand Central Station I saw his book in the paperback novel section of a bookstore. I never did read it.

What I had just heard and witnessed had to be one of the most bizarre things I had ever encountered in my life. If I ever told the story, I would be dismissed as a bull-shit artist. But for some reason, I felt compelled to tell the story. I'd look up my sailor-turned-author.

CHAPTER TWENTY-ONE

October 8
Yacht Reindeer
Hudson River, New York

The small black helicopter came in high and circled the yacht. Seeing it gave me mixed feelings of relief on one hand and new apprehensions on the other. I had to give Steve credit for the skill it took to bring it down on the almost miniature landing pad on the back of the boat. He hovered a few feet in the air for a moment and then, as if taking a chance, dropped onto the deck. The yacht lurched and settled back into the water. Immediately, Steve jumped out and began securing the struts and rotors of the chopper.

Next, out came Howie, moving cautiously, pistol in hand. He waved with his pistol hand for the two passengers to get out. The first passenger was the goateed dog trainer, the other was a much younger man dressed in a bright red jumpsuit. They waited for Steve to finish. Goatee had his hands partially raised in the air. Then, Steve in the lead, followed by Goatee and Jumpsuit, with Howie bringing up the rear, they moved forward to the front of the yacht. I came down from the bridge and met them halfway.

Jumpsuit spoke first. "The situation in Chechnya, while serious, is actually necessary. Historically, the nation has been bound together as a federation not an empire, thus protecting all ethnic, religious, and cultural groups. Therefore, you mother-fucker, rat shit, retard bastard, must incorporate the Chechin experience into rat shit, rat shit, puke, mother-fucker."

"Shut up," Goatee commanded.

"Meet the Pretty Boy," Howie said blandly. "Great-grand-son of the mad monk, Rasputin, and blood-heir to the Russian throne; and, among other things, a sufferer of Turret Syndrome."

"Exactly." Jumpsuit started up again, "We must reach eco-nomic parity with the West and that can only be achieved through rat shit, rat shit, jerk-off bastard."

"Yeah," I said, "And a partridge in a pear tree. Get them upstairs, Howie."

We climbed up to the bridge and went through the salon, passing Whiting's body. Goatee and Jumpsuit took notice but said nothing except for a single "mother-fucker" from the Rus-sian heir. Steve looked a little shocked. Howie simply asked, "What happened to him?"

"I think it was something he ate," I answered. There were no further comments.

We threw Goatee into the galley, quickly securing the door again. In the process, pounding and yelling came from inside with cries of, "Help! Let us out of here! What's going on?" Howie fired a shot high through the door; instantaneously the noise stopped.

We secured the Mad Monk's equally mad great-grandson into a windowless bathroom off the main bedroom suite, having first taken the precaution to remove anything that seemed dan-gerous. As an additional safeguard, we found a length of chain and made it fast to the door.

"He's not going any place," Howie said emphatically. Through the door we could hear bursts of profanity amidst schol-arly treatises of contemporary political analysis.

"Mad as a hatter," Howie said.

"I think it's time to turn these people over to someone. We've taken this as far as we can."

Thankfully, Howie said, "I think you're right. Incidentally, can you handle this boat?"

"Sure. It's been a long time since my Brown Water Navy days but I can bring her in."

Howie asked me for a cigarette; we both lit up. "You know," he said, "that dog handler is some kind of super advance type Pavlovian trainer. They had him train the Crown Prince here so they can wind him up and have him say his piece but that's about it."

Knocking over a chair, Steve burst into the room.. "We've got problems," he spat out, looking very frightened. We followed him back on deck. "Holy shit," exclaimed Howie as he reached for a huge pair of Navy binoculars. Coming up fast behind the yacht were two water ski type speed boats and a small, modern cabin cruiser. Even without the binoculars, I could see that all three boats were manned by heavily armed men. A single man on a Ski-Doo criss-crossed in front of the three boats.

Howie put the binoculars down and turned to me saying, "Well, Jake O'Brien, it looks like you are going to go down in history."

"Yeah? For what?" I could hear the disgust in my own voice.

"It looks like you're going to be the last officer in the history of the U.S. Navy to repel boarders." With that, he stepped into the bridge cabin, emerging again with the Remington. Calmly and very deliberately, he checked the action then lifted the stock slowly to his shoulder. Taking aim, he moved, gradually following his target. The rifle cracked and the figure flew off the Ski-Doo.

Steve looked shocked and asked, "Can we shoot?"

"Goddamn right we can. You take the Kalashnikov and cut

the boats loose from the gangway. Jake, get this thing started."

"Right." I grabbed the shotgun, threw it on top of the control dash and hit the emergency anchor release, simultaneously kicking over the engines. The boat throbbed and I felt us begin slowly moving forward. Gradually, we began to pick up momentum. I steered for the deep water channel.

The sound of heavy firing came from the rear below me - the distinctive rapid sounds of the Kalashnikov, punctuated by the periodic crack of Howie with the Remington.

I locked the wheel and checked outside. Steve was crouched behind the bulkhead, changing the magazine of his weapon. 'I guess Steve found his "Shooting War,"' I thought. He had been pounding rounds into the cabin cruiser. Howie was standing up carefully aiming and picking off occupants in the two smaller speedboats. All three boats were zig-zagging to avoid the fire.

I ducked back into the bridge cabin and grabbed the wheel amid shattering glass and flying wood splinters. My peripheral vision caught sight of one speedboat coming abreast of us on the right. Swerving the wheel hard right, I careened the yacht into the side of the small boat.

Reversing one engine, I swung the wheel to the left and steered into the current. The yacht shuttered and strained but came quickly about, with the help of the current, a full hundred-and-eighty degrees. The aft end slammed against the speedboat, shattering it. It broke up and disappeared. I cut the wheel back, reversed the one engine again and headed for the middle of the river.

Automatic weapons fire began to disintegrate the bridge. As soon as I hit the channel, I turned south and, locking the wheel, hit the deck. Bullets and debris flew around me like deadly hornets but it was the whine of the ricochets that scared the hell out of me. I reached up for the shotgun and crawled out of what was left of the cabin.

I started to slowly lift myself up to look over the bulkhead but never made it. The bright hot flash of an explosion knocked me back. I got to my feet and saw a flaming fountain, like some obscene fireworks display, rising from the water where the cabin cruiser had been. A lucky shot from Steve had hit a fuel tank or something.

I glanced to my left and saw the last boat begin to drop back; it had obviously lost its taste for the pursuit.

Howie lay on the deck below me, propped up against a hatch cover, his left arm limp and bleeding, his pistol loosely held in his right hand, the rifle discarded. I called out to Steve who was already making his way to him.

"Get him up here," I yelled.

Startled by the sound of a new threat, I spun just as a Huey helicopter, bearing the yellow and blue markings of the New York State Police, passed over about twenty feet above us.

"CEASE FIRING. THIS IS THE POLICE. CEASE YOUR FIRING AND DROP YOUR WEAPONS," demanded a voice from its loud speakers.

'Just in time,' I thought cynically. The State Police helicopter then moved to watch us from a safe distance. Surveying the carnage around us, I couldn't blame them.

Downstream I could see a small flotilla of little boats coming our way. Through the heavy binoculars I read their various markings - *Dutchess County Sheriff's Department*. 'The east bank of the river,' I thought. On the other two in red letters read *Ulster County Sheriff's Department*. 'And the west side.' In the center was a larger craft with the distinctive markings of the Coast Guard. It was too small to be a cutter or even a patrol boat. As it drew closer, I made it out to be a buoy tender.

The ship-to-ship radio came alive. "ON THE VESSEL *RE-INDEER*. THIS IS THE COAST GUARD. STAND BY TO BE BOARDED."

I picked up the microphone and thought for a moment, somewhat surprised that it was still operational.

"Negative that, Coast Guard. This is Lieutenant Commander Jake O'Brien, United States Navy Reserve. This vessel has been seized in accordance with Special Executive Order number 212. Do you copy that? If you copy, state your name and rank."

"What the hell is Executive Order 212?" said Howie, who was leaning on Steve in what had been the door of the bridge cabin.

"I don't know," I said. "But he doesn't know either."

The radio came alive again, "Commander, this is Lieutenant J.G. Davis U.S. Coast Guard. Stand by while I await orders."

"Roger, Davis. Did you say Junior Grade?" I asked, emphasizing our difference in rank.

"Affirmative Commander, Junior Grade."

"What's the closest Coast Guard Station, Lieutenant?"

"Saugerties, sir."

"Coast Guard, make way your small boats to pick up survivors, direct police craft to assist, then escort this vessel to Saugerties Station."

The radio went silent. I turned to Howie and Steve. "Did you get hit?" I asked.

"No, Captain Hornblower. When you spun this thing around I got slammed to the deck and broke my arm. I think I snapped a couple of ribs, too. First the damn dog bit me, now you break the same damn arm. There's gotta be an easier way."

"It's a nasty compound fracture," Steve added as he helped Howie to the floor.

"VESSEL *REINDEER* THIS IS THE COAST GUARD. WE HAVE BEEN INSTRUCTED TO ADHERE TO YOUR ORDER AND ESCORT YOU TO COAST GUARD STATION SAUGERTIES." He paused with microphone open, then continued. "Commander, if you attempt evasive action we have been instructed to fire on you."

"Roger that, Coast Guard." I wondered what he intended to fire on us with since he had an unarmed vessel.

We headed down river following Lieutenant J.G. Davis in his buoy tender, leaving the floating carnage to the police and Coast Guard life boats.

CHAPTER TWENTY-TWO

October 8
Yacht Reindeer
Hudson River

It didn't seem to take long before I sighted the Saugerties Point Lighthouse. Howie was slumped in an arm chair nursing a bottle of Hennessey cognac with his good arm. Steve had proved multi-talented and had put a rather professional splint and bandage on Howie's broken left arm. But now he was pacing in a wired hyper state, in and out of what had been the bridge cabin door. I was surprised but not really concerned that Howie had fallen off the wagon and was drinking again.

We rounded the point and headed up the mouth of the Esopus River. I closely followed the young J.G. in his buoy tender. He knew the channel, which was none too wide and our boat drew a lot of water. I slowed to almost a crawl.

I had sent Steve back to bring up Mr. Turret Syndrome and Howie rallied and went with him. In a few moments Howie was back, in his good hand was a red nylon jumpsuit. "Well, Jake, my boy, I've got some bad news." He handed me the jumpsuit and reached for the cognac.

"What's going on?" I asked, dropping the jumpsuit, not wanting to be distracted from what was becoming tricky navigation.

"I don't know how to put this," he said.

"Shut up and just tell me." I was surprised at my sharp tone.

Howie, not taking offense, replied, "The Mad Hatter's gone. The door was locked and the chain was still fast, like the way we left it but, well, the bathroom was empty, well, except for this," pointing to the jumpsuit on the floor with the cognac bottle.

"He can't be gone, there was no way out and it wasn't that long ago we locked him up; he's got to be here. Look around for him."

"I've got Steve doing that now, as we speak."

"Talk about having explaining to do. It was bad enough when we had him, but now..." At that moment Steve appeared in the door. "I checked everyplace except the galley. I went pretty fast but there aren't a lot of places to hide on this thing. Do you want Howie and me to go back and check again?"

"No, there's no time. You didn't check the galley?"

"No," Steve said, "I tried the door; it was still locked and as soon as I did the people inside started yelling again."

Up ahead was the Coast Guard Station, such as it was. It appeared to have only one deep water dock. I was surprised it even had that, considering the fact that the Esopus was little more than a creek. The buoy tender pulled away and indicated that we should pull alongside the one mooring position. The dock virtually teemed with men, many of them armed with rifles and shotguns. A few were uniformed Coast Guardsmen, but mostly they were people in suits and ties wearing blue jackets emblazoned with *FBI* in yellow letters; a few jackets said *Customs*. Police in various types of uniforms mingled in the crowd with other nondescript types. On the bank, behind the dock, were an assortment of official vehicles, all with their lights flashing. I was glad to see at least one ambulance - Howie's arm was pretty bad.

"Look," I said, "you two get the prisoners out of the galley and get them down to the aft deck, and for God's sake, keep an eye on them."

"Right," they both said in unison as they started out of the shattered door.

"And," I continued, "keep an eye out for the missing Russian heir."

I was less than fifty yards off the dock, mostly letting the current take me in, when Howie popped back in, Remington rifle tucked under his broken arm. I glanced to the rear of the boat and saw the little group huddled together with their hands on their heads. Steve, a few feet away from them, covered them with his Kalashnikov.

I turned back to see Howie fiddling with the P.A. system by the boat's radio. "Ah," he said, pushing some buttons, "I found this C.D. by the entertainment center in the salon."

I was concentrating on bringing in the boat but managed to glance at the C.D. case he was holding up - *The Best of Jefferson Airplane*. Howie discarded the case and slung the heavy Navy binoculars around his neck. Then, picking up the cognac bottle, hurried out.

I was almost to the dock when the strains of "White Rabbit" began to scream forth from the yacht's loud speakers. I looked back to see Howie standing on top of the salon cabin roof. How the hell he got there was beyond me. But there he was, in all his glory - broken arm and all - resplendent with rifle and binoculars, drinking freely from the cognac bottle. To the lyric, "...one pill makes you larger..." the yacht hit the dock, causing the last of the shattered glass to fall from the bridge's windows. We were some sight.

Skilled young Coast Guardsmen threw ropes and lines and made us fast. Like ants, the blue jacketed FBI agents swarmed over the bulkhead and dispersed throughout the boat. There seemed to be no end of them. I was shutting down the engines and other systems when some of them got to the bridge.

"FBI, Mr. O'Brien. You're under arrest."

"What for?"

One leveled a shotgun at my mid-section and demanded, "Get your hands up and we will take that weapon."

"I don't think so," Howie said, appearing in the shattered door behind me, sans Remington and cognac, his pistol in hand down at this side.

"You, too, Littlepage, drop that piece."

Silence began a long, tense moment. It was broken by an authoritative, deep gruff voice. "Stand aside. Let me through. Get out of the way." Pushing into the cabin was a grey haired, slender man in his mid-sixties, dressed in a decades old sports jacket. Beside him, I was relieved to see a familiar face - Attorney David Jeffries.

"Put that thing away," he commanded in an insulting way to the agent with the shotgun. Appearing into view in the back of what was now becoming a crowd, was a smartly uniformed Navy Lieutenant wearing the braid of an Admiral's aide.

"Who the hell are you?" demanded the FBI agent who seemed to be in charge, "And who let these people through?" he said, raising on his toes and peering about looking for a negligent, responsible person. He spotted the Admiral's aide.

"I am Rear Admiral Jonathan Cutter, United States Navy and this is Attorney David Jeffries, Special Counsel to the Defense Intelligence Agency."

"Well, this is an FBI matter."

"The hell it is," the Admiral shot back.

The agent with the shotgun lowered it; clearly the FBI was losing ground. "These men are under arrest."

"What are they being charged with?" Jeffries quietly asked.

"Piracy, for all I know. We'll let the U.S. Attorney's Office figure that out. You have no jurisdiction here, Admiral."

"Of course, I do. Explain to him why, Jeffries."

"Well, Mr. O'Brien here is a United States Naval Officer who, while acting in his official capacity, seized this vessel operating in tidal waters; it was involved in highly classified international matters adverse to American interests and Mr. Littlepage assisted in this as an agent for his firm which has been retained by the Defense Intelligence Agency."

"Crap," said the senior FBI man. "O'Brien retired a month ago. He's a civilian now."

"Well?" said the Admiral, turning to Jeffries.

"That was part of Mr. O'Brien's cover. Yes, he retired from the Naval Investigative Service but his Reserve Commission has been activated. Isn't that correct, Mr. O'Brien?"

Not wanting to interfere with the lawyer's flow which, frankly, was pretty good, I took the easy way out. "I am not at liberty to discuss that at this time."

Silence reigned again as another tense stand-off ensued. This one was broken by the Admiral's aide stepping forward with a small cell phone in his hand. "Sir," he said, "I have the FBI Director's Office on the line."

The Admiral in mufti grabbed the phone, which looked too small for him, and put it to his ear. "Admiral Cutter here."

"Yes, yes, yes. I see, yes. Very good." The Admiral was sounding very official but through the officialdom, the satisfaction in his voice was clear. He handed the phone to the boss FBI agent. Our side was clearly winning.

The FBI man began to verbally weave and bob, "Yes, I understand. But of course. No question. Yes, sir. Etc., etc..." He pushed the phone antenna back into the unit and handed it to the Admiral's aide.

"Uh hum," the agent cleared his throat. "I have been directed to put my men at your disposal, Admiral. Mr. O'Brien and Littlepage are free to go."

"Admiral, how about Steve Richards? He was taken off in handcuffs; he's one of my men," said Howie.

The agent jerked his head and a lessor-type agent was dispensed to extricate Steve. It was not even necessary for Jeffries to invent an official status for him. I was sure Jeffries was probably thankful for that.

In an almost patronizing tone of voice, the Admiral informed the FBI agents that there was glory enough to go around and the FBI would be given the honor of making dozens of arrests around the country of individuals, some of whom quite prominent, that were involved in all manner of crimes and conspiracies against the government.

As if to underscore his victory, Admiral Cutter turned to me and said, "There will be a decoration in this for you, O'Brien."

"Thank you, sir. Littlepage is hurt pretty bad. I'd like to see him get to a hospital."

"Of course, of course. Let's move out."

The Admiral, with his aide and Jeffries, cleared the way for me to help Howie down from the shattered bridge and over the bulkhead to the dock. Before getting to the ambulance, a blue-jacketed Customs man stepped in front of us and demanded Howie's newly acquired binoculars. Howie insisted that they were really his but to no avail. With great reluctance, he surrendered them. The Admiral and Lawyer Jeffries were of no help. I guessed it was okay to commandeer yachts, shoot people and blow up boats but, well, taking binoculars, that was out of the question.

An FBI agent and the Admiral's aide got into the back with Howie. As the ambulance pulled away with Howie strapped to the gurney, I heard him say, "Jake, this is what you've got to do," before the attendant swung the doors shut.

Pondering on what his parting advice might have been, I turned and, lighting a cigarette, took one last look at the yacht *Reindeer*. A couple of Customs agents, one with the binoculars in his hand, were pasting stickers on the side of the boat in bold letters: **"SEIZED BY THE U.S. CUSTOMS SERVICE."**

CHAPTER TWENTY-THREE

October 31
All Hallows' Eve

The Frank Lloyd Wright house, shrouded in darkness, clung to the hillside in the woods above the Potomac River. In it the five remaining Council members met. They sat evenly spaced at the round slate table. Their new council chamber was a stone and glass room suspended over the waterfall created by the small stream which cascaded down the precipice to the river below.

He finished his report, closing the folder in front of him, and concluded by saying, "Therefore it has been absolutely confirmed that our seven, shall we say, more dedicated, members departed this life, either by their own hand or heroically while resisting arrest either in this country or in Russia. As a result of their deaths, our identities remain unknown to anyone outside of this room. Lastly, while we have lost almost all of our contacts here and abroad, our financial resources have been left virtually intact."

"Not so bad," said the man in the grey suit, "fewer members, less overhead mean..."

"More for each of us. For heaven's sake, how much would be enough for you, anyway?" said another man. "We should concentrate on rebuilding our organization so that when the time comes, really comes, we will be in a position to move."

"Don't act so pious," he answered. "You were right there in our decision to eliminate our more fanatical brothers who believed that the time had come."

"Stop bickering, will you? Let's move on. Internal conflict on the Council is both unproductive and dangerous."

"Look who's talking. You cut it pretty close; your plan was pretty chancy."

"Chancy? I don't think so. I knew my brother, the great Admiral Samuel Jeffries, would do his damnedest to destroy us once we invited him for membership. It was then just a question of controlling and focusing the damage."

****

The serpentine driveway of the house blended into the natural landscape and entered onto the access road which wound its way down the side of the hill. Along the road were a few other custom houses, all picturesquely situated behind shrubs, ornamental trees, and some large, old, standing oaks. Somehow, Fairfax County, Virginia, had maintained not simply a suburban but rather a rural, almost wilderness, environment even though it was virtually next to the urban sprawl of Washington D.C.

We sat in a rented car concealed in the driveway of a large Colonial house whose owners were apparently away on vacation, or at least we hoped they were.

"They've been up there a long time, Howie. What the heck could they be up to?"

"I don't know but I suspect we're going to find out. Anyway, we can't miss him. He's got to come back down this road." Howie paused for a moment and, still staring straight ahead through the windshield, asked, "What got you into the spy business, anyway Jake? In a lot of ways, you're not the type. You know - Notre Dame, commissioned as a line officer, middle class guy - no, you're not the type."

"It just sorta happened, you know, I went from sailor to spy to Navy cop. I think the truth of it, Howie, was, after my first tour in Vietnam, I was tainted. If I had realized that then I would have gotten out and done something different."

"What do you mean 'tainted'?"

"Well, my first tour I was an Ensign and commanded a PBR. Actually, I commanded a four boat unit of PBRs. I worked out of an old LST anchored down by the mouth of the Mekong."

"Yeah, that's right. That night back on the river, you said something about the Brown Water Navy. PBR - Patrol Boat River."

"Or, as we called 'em - 'The Proud, The Brave, The Reliable' - good old Admiral Zumwalt's private little navy."

"You guys did a pretty good job, so why the tarnish?"

"We were too close in to the ground action with the Army. Working the river was dirty, dangerous, counterinsurgency type of stuff, real nasty on both sides. It sure wasn't like sittin' on an aircraft carrier or battleship with its sixteen-inch guns sitting off the coast. Once you spent some time on the river, they didn't want you back."

"So they moved you over to ONI which, on the surface, would seem logical."

"Yeah, looking back on it, I realize that working the river before my lateral move over to intelligence shaped my thinking. I guess it made me more than a little cynical. I did my job. I did it well but I was never out to screw anybody unless they really deserved it. And, someplace in the back of my mind, I always figured the system was out to screw me."

"Hey Jake, that's him," Howie interjected as a car shot down the road a dozen yards in front of us.

"Are you sure?"

"Yeah. No mistaking that Jag," Howie said as he started the car.

"Let's go," I said impulsively as Howie pulled out onto the road.

Some training but a lot of experience allowed Howie to stay close enough to the Jag to keep it in sight but far enough away to keep from being detected. Howie drove focused on the Jag. I worked as navigator, keeping Howie posted with, "The light's turning red...Watch out for the intersection...There's a car passing you on the left...Watch out for the cop up there..."

Eventually, the two cars entered onto Rock Creek Parkway.

"Chevy Chase, Jake; he's headed for home."

"I think so. Wanna take the chance?"

"Okay, let's back off and in twenty minutes check his driveway."

Twenty minutes later we rode by the driveway of the opulent but tasteful house with the late model Jaguar parked in the driveway.

"There it is, Howie, he's in there."

"Yup. What time do you have?"

"Eleven-thirty. Let's wait 'til a little after midnight to go in."

"A little preparation pays off. Whadaya say we go in the French doors to the library like we did this afternoon?"

"Works for me," I replied.

The hall clock chimed twelve-thirty as Howie sat down behind the large desk in the formal library. I was pouring a drink from a rolling bar in the corner.

"Can I fix you somethin', Howie?"

"No thanks, Jake. I'm back on the wagon."

"You don't mind if I do?"

"No, but make sure you drink the good stuff."

"This guy's got nothing but good stuff."

Slowly and cautiously David Jeffries came down the staircase in the hallway. He was wearing silk pajamas and a brocade bathrobe, his right hand thrust into the pocket.

Howie looked up from the desk. "Ah, David, I was wondering how much noise we had to make before we brought you downstairs. By the way, take your hand out of the pocket, very slowly, or you're dead where you stand."

With confidence and bravado, Jeffries replied, "Well, I have to give you two more credit that I had thought." He took his hand from the pocket of his robe.

"Something to drink, Counselor?" I said from the corner.

"Why not? Whiskey, neat, if you please."

I poured a good measure of Scotch into the Waterford crystal tumbler, walked to the library doorway where he was now standing and handed him the glass. I reached into the bathrobe pocket, removing the small but deadly Mauser pistol, and walked over and put it on the desk in front of Howie.

"Sit down, Champ," said Howie, displaying his 9mm Beretta in a pointing motion towards a high-back chair.

The attorney Jeffries complied, casting a condescending glance toward Howie, obviously annoyed at his intentionally disrespectful demeanor.

I sat in a matching chair across from him.

"Answer me one thing, if you would," spat Jeffries. "How did you know?"

"It didn't take a mental giant to figure it out," I said.

"Obviously not," responded Jeffries as he raised his glass.

"Look, Champ,"Howie said, "if you're so smart, how come I've got the gun?" Howie was getting annoyed; there was a dangerous silence for a moment.

Looking for words, I said, "The common denominator, motive, opportunity."

The silence broken, I continued, "Look, your brother was set up. Granted, the heart attack just happened but nonetheless, he was set up and it had to be somebody close to him. Your motive for wanting Howie and me to keep a lid on this thing was a little weak. You showed up at every point in this thing and you had the motive."

"Yes, but what was that motive?" asked Jeffries smugly, sipping his whiskey.

"I don't know," said Howie, "but you have a motive, whatever it is, and the proof of it is that you were always there to clean everything up and make it right, even that day on the river. So, I don't have to know the motive, I just gotta know you have one."

"Yeah," I said, "and the fact you had the ability to clean everything up."

Jeffries silently chuckled and placed his drink on the small table next to him. "It was really quite transparent, wasn't it?" he said now, without any hint of arrogance in his voice.

"Now, to quote Paul Harvey," Howie said "'What's the rest of the story?' What was your motive? It sure wasn't what that lunatic, Whiting, was babbling about - putting some descendant of Rasputin back on the throne."

"No, while that was an element, our, or my, goals are somewhat more, shall we say, grandiose."

"What I'm real interested in is how the Aryan Brotherhood fits into this Russian monarchy crap and, for some strange reason, I got a feeling you're gonna tell us."

"Why not," said Jeffries, lifting his glass, "at this point we have already started controlled leaks to the media; you know, let the people have just enough information to satisfy them. Besides, it's an interesting tale, worth telling, even though it's quite simple." Jeffries took a generous drink from his glass and set it down. Hesitating as he reached for the cigarette box and lighter on the table, "May I?" he asked, making eye contact with Howie, who nodded in approval. Jeffries lit a cigarette, inhaled deeply and settled back.

"Everybody in the business knows that in 1945, contrary to the Potsdam Agreement with the Soviets, the United States Army recruited top Nazi intelligence officers who had worked in, or as in the case of General Gehlen, who was actually in charge of, German Intelligence regarding the Soviet Union and Eastern Europe. It was really like something out of Kafka, these Nazis were kept in a luxury Prisoner of War camp and simply continued their intelligence operations against the East, for the United States instead of Hitler. At the same time, with a little less luxury and sophistication, the Soviets were doing the same thing against the U.S. out of East Germany."

"That," interjected Howie, "I could have gotten from the History Channel. Let's move this along a little bit."

"And spare us the morality lecture that it was simply just an expedient and pragmatic measure ," I added.

"Perhaps for the moment," Jeffries continued, "but the theory was flawed. Since both Soviet and American Intelligence regarding Eastern, and for that matter most of, Europe was being run by former German officers, eventually these old comrades, who had not lost their Nazi ideology, had to come to an accommodation with each other. It was only natural. It could be said, having lost the Second World War, they decided to win, or at least profit from, the Cold War. Both sides impressed their new employers-slash-sponsors by the quality of the information they were developing. What neither side realized was that these entrepreneurs were collaborating for the most part...simply exchanging information."

"No wonder the Cold War escalated so quickly," I heard myself saying.

"Exactly," Jeffries stated, stabbing out his cigarette for emphasis. "In fact, many of the crises of the Cold War were contrived by these now-Chiefs of Intelligence, simply to guarantee their positions."

"Okay," Howie said, somewhat condescendingly, "we're doing better. So that part isn't on the History Channel but it still isn't totally new. How do we get to Rasputin, Rasputin's grandkids, and the Neo-Nazis?"

"Look," Jeffries said, showing a little frustration, "all countries, all societies, particularly the power-elite of those societies, have some real or imagined, rational or irrational, mystical imperative that grants their right to rule. When the belief in the Divine Right of Monarchs began to dissolve, the mystics with their secret societies, rituals, and supposedly hidden knowledge, came forward to replace it."

"It's incredibly obvious but the average person doesn't see it," said Jeffries, with a tone indicating his amazement at how so many had missed the obvious. He continued, "Everyone overlooks the mystical, occult nature of the Nazi movement, which is one of the reasons that allows it to still exist, and in a very meaningful way."

"And a Rasputin-Romanov heir does the same thing for Russia today?" Howie asked.

"Something like that," Jeffries answered, clearly becoming somewhat bored by the conversation.

"But it seems to me," I said, "that a Russian mystical system and a Nazi mystical system are somewhat incompatible.

"Only on the surface, Mr. O'Brien, only on the surface. In the final analysis, how much of a difference is there between Stalin and Hitler and, thus, between Rasputin and Himmler? At a point in time, the Soviet government reached the same conclusion the Germans had."

"Which was?" I asked.

"What the corrupting influences of the world were - the mixing of the pure white race with the mongrels of the world, the corrupting influences of the humans without souls and the continued threat of the Jews and the Zionists, be they in Moscow, Zurich or Wall Street."

"Ah, the Jews, Jake, the Jews. Whatever would we do without the Jews to blame things on?" threw in Howie.

"So, let's wrap this up," I said. "The Neo-Nazi thing is the American chapter of all of this."

"Component, Mr. O'Brien, component. I prefer to think of the Aryan Order Brotherhood as being the American component. Germany played its rôle in exterminating the undesirables, the Soviet Union, or Russia, was even more successful, and now it is time for those of pure blood, in spirit and thought, to purify this country which is rapidly becoming a mongrel refuge."

"Okay, that's it," said Howie. "I'll tell you one thing, for all of our incompetence, I don't think it's gonna be all that easy for this council of yours to continue to operate in this country."

With an air of great authority, Jeffries held up his hand and said, "No? I think it is simply time for us to move our base of operations to some, shall we say, more conducive climate, where we will continue to function with relative anonymity."

"Where might that be?" I asked.

"Oh, now, Mr. O'Brien, that would be telling," said Jeffries coyly. "Let me suggest, perhaps, Japan, a powerful economic force seeking to re-assert itself internationally and with its own tradition of mysticism, complete with a god-emperor. Perhaps China; now that the Communist dynasty has collapsed, they are seeking a new national identity backed up by some moral dictate. Australia is even a possibility... But let me ask you a question."

"Okay," I said.

"Why were you so fanatical, so relentless, in pursuing this? It wasn't your job. It's not loyalty to your country. I really don't think it was money. What was it?"

"Rossi. Mike Rossi. I'm not sure that we were friends in the normal sense. We were partners in the official sense but I think I owed it to him. I think my relationship to him contained my last vestige of loyalty to anyone or anything."

"Rossi? But who was this Mike Rossi?"

I felt not rage, but a dream-like quality, almost an out-of-body experience, as I stood up and pointed my still-rented .45 automatic at the usually well-assured but now confused lawyer.

I heard the first shot and saw Jeffries' head jerk back; the second impacted his chest and he careened forward like a crash-test dummy. I absently looked on at my un-fired gun. I began to awake from my trance-like state as I looked over to Howie, who was quickly wiping off Jeffries' Mauser pistol. Howie casually tossed the Mauser onto the floor next to Jeffries' body. I felt him take me by the arm and propel me out the French doors through which we had entered.

I contemplated the events of the evening as we drove north in silence. A few miles from Jeffries' house would have placed us in downtown Washington where shootings and killings over drug deals are relentlessly pursued by the police. Murder in that area can, and frequently does, result in the death penalty but yet, I knew there was no jeopardy here. The killing of a well-connected, wealthy, Washington-area lawyer might, at most, result in a back page newspaper footnote regarding his suicide. In all likelihood, not even that would happen. As in the previous violence I had recently witnessed, somebody from somewhere under someone's orders would clean everything up.

I think the adrenalin rush that had to hit me at Jeffries' house, followed by the profound silence in the car as we drove during the early morning hours, cleared my brain and crystallized my thoughts.

Jeffries never did say what specifically motivated him. But to use his term, he became quite transparent. Sure, his machinations gave him access to wealth, and therefore, a luxurious lifestyle. Sure, there were the status, the privilege and the social connections but, for all of his polish, education, and sophistication, in the final analysis, he was nothing more than a bully. And the elixir of life for bullies is the ability to exercise power, pure power, over others. The history of the world has been filled with megalomaniac bullies - the Napoleons, the Hitlers, the Mussolinis, the Stalins. The famous ones, interestingly enough, have been the least clever for they have not been able to suppress their own need for public ego gratification, a fault which is usually their undoing. It was the Jeffries' of the world, though, who really understood power and that the basis of their power was in secrecy. They were the controllers from behind the scenes. They were the ones through banks, industry, corrupt bureaucracies and all other institutions of civilization, who shaped and molded national and international policy for their own purposes. They had no need for banners, torch-lit parades, or mass rallies but, nonetheless, profoundly influenced the lives of the average man on the street, for whom they had no respect. Jeffries was undoubtedly a racist and a classist but to what degree he bought into some esoteric mysticism that surrounded his "Council," I could only speculate.

It wasn't until we were crossing the Delaware Memorial Bridge into New Jersey that Howie and I spoke.

"Why did you do it?" I asked.

"Because you wouldn't. And what were we gonna do, call the police and tell them they ought to arrest Rasputin's grandson or something?"

"I would have done it, Howie."

"Yeah, you might have but you would have felt bad about it the moment you pulled the trigger so that's why I pulled the trigger."

"And what did you feel?"

"The recoil of my weapon."

We didn't speak again for the rest of the drive back to New York.

EPILOGUE

*"We do not have to visit a madhouse to find disor-
dered minds. Our planet is the mental institution of
the universe."*

Johann Wolfgang Von Goethe

Howie called last night while Françoise and I were packing up the shop. Everything in the shop was being shipped to a dealer in South Carolina I had wholesaled it to. We were thankful for the interruption in the tedium of boxing and loading the ten rooms of antiques, bric-a-brac, and furniture. But it would have been good to hear from him anyway.

He said he was touring the Midwest inspecting a chain of gas station/convenience stores for his security company. Part of the inspection included interrogating the employees for cash register theft and pilferage. I hoped he kept things in perspective and didn't wind up shooting anyone. Anyway, he sounded good and said he called to see if I had gotten the newspaper article he had sent me. Even though I had, Howie insisted on reading it to me again over the telephone.

> REUTERS: MOSCOW *A new cult has entered the already crowded playing field in a Russia which seems to be desperately embracing every form of religious revivalism since the fall of Communism. Six cities which loosely orbit Moscow, known as Zolotoye Koltso, or Golden Ring, comprised a pilgrimage route in pre-Revolutionary Russia. A self-proclaimed monk calling himself Grigory Romanov and purporting to be a descendant of Rasputin, has revived the tradition of this pilgrimage. This monk has attracted a significant following, largely due to his 1960's-type philosophy of free sex.*

Howie finished the article with great satisfaction. "So, what do you think?" he asked. "Is it or isn't it our guy?"

"Actually, I hope it is," I said. "I don't want to think that someone's cloning these wackos."

Françoise got on the phone with Howie and with a great deal of almost childlike glee told him that she made her last performance as a working girl and, with the benefit of the legendary casting couch, she had landed a pretty decent part in an upcoming movie. My satisfaction was derived from the fact that her partner on the couch was none other than my ex-wife's screenwriter housemate, Frank Dunlop. I should say, ex-housemate 'cause JoAnne threw him out, bag and baggage, of course blaming me for their break up. So, what else is new?

You didn't need a cryptologist to tell from their conversation that she was going to be joining Howie on his road trip across America. Hopefully, Françoise would help to keep his interrogation techniques from getting out of hand, and maybe he could pry the secret of her background from her.

Speaking of cryptologists, Howie seemed pleased when I told him that the Rev. Jeanette Quinlan had been appointed the Head Chaplain at the Federal Corrections Institution in Otisville, New York. While the Feds were willing to provide her with housing, she opted for a car instead and chose to commute from the Astoria Hotel. We both wondered if she would end up ministering to any of the people we were responsible for putting away.

On a more personal note, I thanked Howie for his advice to Rachel. He had told her, when she visited him in the hospital, "Here's what you've got to do - get out on your own and see the world." In a convoluted but evidently effective presentation, he advised her to enroll in Trinity College in Dublin to get in touch with her roots. "And they also have a great women's program," he said. Then he added, "Try to find an opportunity to get to know your father."

I told Howie, who was not surprised to hear, that my nebulous status with the Navy had been clarified. It seems that my retirement papers had never actually been correctly processed so I was still officially an active member of the Naval Investigative Service.

"What a coincidence!" he said.

Undoubtedly for appearance sake, I was being called back for six months of uniformed service, conveniently out of the country at what was described as some soft post. Truthfully, it made me feel clean to be back in whites again. Plus I was getting kicked up to Full Commander; the added time and grade would boost my eventual pension considerably.

I told Howie that when I got back I was going to convert the shop into a Bed and Breakfast. I had had enough of being described as a used furniture salesman. He said he would refer business to me and visit himself on occasion. I met that with mixed emotions. One thing I realized during my limited partnership with Howie Littlepage was that, while I could change my behavior and lifestyle to a certain degree, I couldn't pretend to be something that I was not. I was a cop. A Navy cop, maybe, but a cop nonetheless. I had a cop's mentality. I could be a cop or a retired cop running a Bed and Breakfast and, actually, I felt pretty good about that.

We ended the conversation assuring each other that we would keep in touch. I had the feeling we would.

****

I had to laugh when I opened the mail today; my orders from the Navy came through. I was being posted for six months as Deputy Naval Attache, an intelligence slot, in, of all places, Dublin. Can you imagine that?

192

AUTHOR'S NOTE

Russia had teetered on the brink of revolution for decades but the event of the First World War in 1914 is what disrupted the delicate balance and plunged the Tsarist government into the abyss. While the "Great War" was the coup de grace, a number of other events combined to cause the ultimate collapse of Russia. Rasputin has been credited as one of the chief factors.

For a number of critical years, Tsar Nicholas had unquestioning faith in the monk's counsel, much of which was ill-advised. Equally destructive were the Court and political intrigues in which Rasputin involved himself. The widespread rumors, which may have been well-founded, that Rasputin was a German agent, seriously undermined the Tsarist government but it was the accepted fact that he was sexually involved with the Empress, and possibly some of the Royal daughters, that was most damaging. In short, it destroyed the purity, both religious and secular, of the Imperial Family and its right to rule in the eyes and hearts of the Russian people. The Russian soldier is perhaps the most patriotic in the world and has always fought to the death for Mother Russia but once he came to believe that the Empress was a harlot, sleeping with a German agent, he laid down his rifle, left the trenches, and simply walked home.

Revolution and the collapse of the monarchy brought on civil war throughout the former Russian Empire. The violence raged from the Ukraine to the Urals to the far Pacific city of Vladivostock. History has chosen, except for the Russians, to forget the extensive and bloody military intervention in that civil war by the United States, Britain, and other European powers.

Ultimately, Communism, or more correctly Lenin, prevailed and the former Russian Empire was transformed into the Soviet Union. The Romanov Tsars were replaced by new Tsars - Lenin, Stalin, Khrushchev.

The Tsarist regime was not simply a system of government but rather an all-encompassing belief system which was deeply held by all Russians. Perhaps because of this, Russian Communism adopted the same persona. Communism in Russia transcended beyond an economic/political system and became, like the Tsarist regime, a totalist belief system. This multi-faceted belief system touched every aspect of the Soviet citizen's life. In short, it became a religion.

All nations, particularly dictatorships, seek to destroy enemies which pose a threat to the State. This is particularly true of states established around religious or totalist belief systems, witness the Islamic revolutions.

The most dangerous enemies to the religious state are enemies that attack the basic belief system. Most nations employ the use of secret police/intelligence agencies. But the totalist state goes one step further, establishing what amounts to Orwellian "Thought Police." The Nazis had their political police, the Gestapo; the radical Islamic states have their Religious Police; the Soviet Union had the Committee for State Security, the KGB.

The central purpose of the KGB (and its predecessor the NKVD) was to identify and eliminate politically incorrect thinkers that were disruptive to the belief system, thus its obsession with tracking down and assassinating Trotsky. A fellow Communist and revolutionary, Trotsky's crime was that his beliefs differed somewhat from the Party Line, in short he was a heretic.

The ultimate, if not unrealistic, threat to the Russian Communist government was the haunting spectre of the Romanovs.

So real was this threat in the minds of Soviet leaders that whole sections of the KGB were devoted to monitoring and neutralizing any hint of a Romanov return. It was not inconceivable to imagine that the Tsar and/or any number of his family had escaped execution. Some troops did remain loyal to the Tsar. Bribery and rival revolutionary factions and the confusion of the times all could have facilitated their escape.

Similarly, rumors always persisted that the monk, Rasputin, survived the final assassination attempt against him, even though he had been poisoned, stabbed, shot, bludgeoned, and thrown into the frozen Neva River. As with Hitler, for years there were sightings of Rasputin purportedly living in various countries.

If Rasputin did not survive, three of his children by his legitimate wife, Praskovie, did. A fourth child, a son who was labeled a mental defect, died under questionable circumstances. Rasputin's daughter, Maria, married Boris Soloviev, the son of the Treasurer of the Russian Orthodox Church. Soloviev had abandoned Russia to live and work in Germany for a time before traveling to India to study at an esoteric school under the women mystic, Madame Blavatskaya, a fellow Russian expatriate. Madame Blavatskaya provided the spiritual/philosophical framework for the German Nazi Party to the degree of even providing them with the swastika as a mystical symbol. Soloviev later went on to establish a semi-secret society to save members and descendants of the Romanov Family so they later could be returned to the throne.

Western intelligence agencies, particularly the U.S. CIA, were of course aware of the Soviets' concerns regarding a Royalist return. In the black-and-white thinking of the Cold War, whatever concerned the Soviets interested the West.

As a consequence of this, there developed two factions in the CIA. Except for the issues of Imperial Russian gold and other wealth stored in the West and the question of some governments in exile of republics which comprised the Soviet Union and certain other pragmatic issues, the first faction considered a Royalist return as ludicrous. But nonetheless, this faction found leaking rumors and creating elaborate ruses useful in mis-directing and occupying Soviet intelligence operatives.

The other faction, which to a degree, worked in tandem with the first faction, believed that at the right time producing a legitimate and credible Romanov heir would be a powerful weapon in destabilizing the Soviet government.

At a point in time, the search on both sides became something akin to a modern Quest for the Holy Grail. From time to time, stories circulated that one, several, or all of Tsar Nicholas' immediate family had escaped and that they and/or their direct descendants were being secretly supported, protected and groomed by the U.S. government. Not infrequently, these stories included references to mysterious Russian compounds on Long Island, New York.

The break-up of the Soviet Union has brought about a dangerously unstable and violent atmosphere in Russia and Eastern Europe. Numbers of factions in the East and the West have quietly promoted a Royalist return to establish a limited monarchy in that troubled part of the world. Such a monarchy could unite and stabilize the area, giving a national identity to the diverse ethnic groups. It would also provide the Russian government with much needed historical and moral authority.

Newspapers have reported various potential "Royals" have been quietly returning to Mother Russia. Teams of historians and scientists have also headed for Russia. One prestigious collection of forensics experts opened the common grave containing the bodies of the executed Royal Family of Nicholas and Alexandra. The pathologists and DNA experts positively identified six of the bodies of the Imperial Family. One mystery was solved - that being the legend of Anastasia, who was most often rumored to have survived. Sadly, she was there. But a new mystery was born. While there was the body of a boy of about thirteen years, it was definitely not the body of Alexis, the Crown Prince.

Underscoring the popular and mystical fascination with the Romanovs, and seemingly addressing a deep-seated yearning for the national identity of Imperial Russia, a ceremony was planned to re-inter the remains, with the exception of the mystery boy, in the crypt of St. Peter's Church in the ancient Peter and Paul Fortress. However, this has not yet taken place and President Yeltsin has decreed that Lenin will not be buried until the Royal Family has been given a proper burial.

To be buried with the Empress and all four of her daughters are the lockets containing hand-painted pictures of Rasputin which they were wearing when they perished.